Wildfire and
St

STAR MAGE SAGA BOOK 3

J.J. GREEN

ISBN: 978-1-913476-09-0

Sign up to my reader group for a free copy of the Star Mage Saga prequel, Star Mage Exile, discounts on new releases, review team invitations and other interesting stuff:

https://jjgreenauthor.com/free-books/

CONTENTS

Books of the Star Mage Saga

Prequel: Star Mage Exile

Book 1: Daughter of Discord

Book 2: Dark Mage Rises

Book 3: Wildfire and Steel

Book 4: Mercenary Mage

Book 5: Accursed Space

Book 6: Flight From Sanctuary

CHAPTER ONE

Ostillon was at war. The Sherrerrs were attacking the Dirksens' base planet, and Carina and her siblings were running out of places to hide.

For days they had traveled from refuge to refuge, fearing the collapse of their latest home from bombardment, or that Castiel was on their tail. They had not seen their Dark Mage brother, however, and for the moment the bombing had stopped.

"We have to try to find some food, Bryce," said Carina to her friend. "The kids haven't eaten since yesterday."

"I know," he replied. "Let's go now while it's quiet."

They had discovered a basement in an abandoned house the previous day, and with practised ease Carina's siblings had made the place as comfortable as was possible. Parthenia and the twins, Oriana and Ferne, had dragged rugs down from the upper floors, and Nahla had made it her job to furnish the place with cushions.

The mage children and their non-mage sister, Nahla, were keeping themselves occupied with quiet games. The youngest sibling, Darius had found a pack of playing cards and was arranging them face upward in rows. To avoid discovery by their brother, they knew they had to remain inconspicuous. But children's games would not put food in their bellies.

Carina asked her oldest sister, Parthenia, to watch the younger children. Parthenia agreed, as she was always quick to help in whatever way she could. Carina and Bryce climbed the stairs from the basement and emerged in the kitchen. The pantry and cupboards had been the first place they had searched when they arrived, but the food storage spaces were predictably empty.

The war had thrown Ostillon into chaos. All the regular systems of food distribution had broken down, and people had to take whatever they could find. Carina had not figured out what she would do when the day came that she couldn't feed her siblings.

After checking that the street was deserted, Carina and Bryce passed through the front door, which had jammed open due to its warped door frame. They ran to the end of the street on the shadowed side where the rays of the rising sun hadn't reached. While they searched for food someone would eventually see them, but it was important that no one guessed where they'd come from. The last thing she wanted was someone snooping in their hideout while she was gone. It was the best she could do to protect those she had to leave behind.

They headed out of the residential area and toward the nearest commercial district. They had to travel on foot. Carina could have unlocked a vehicle with a Cast, but no working autocars were to be found. Anyone with the ability to leave the city had driven away days previously.

Carina spotted the bombed-out bakery from halfway down the street. The building's ruins were still smoldering from the most recent attack, but looters had already infiltrated the place. She could see shadows of figures moving inside the broken remains. If she and Bryce didn't go inside soon there wouldn't be anything left to scavenge.

She nudged Bryce with her elbow and pointed.

"I see it," he said.

They crossed the road and sped up their pace. Carina hoped no one would give them any trouble. Usually, if plenty of goods remained, there was no fighting. Everyone took as much as they could carry and quickly departed. But if most of the goods had been taken people grew belligerent and things got physical. Carina wasn't bothered by the prospect of fighting the Ostillonian citizens, who were not trained military, but she didn't want to have to hurt anyone.

As they arrived at the demolished bakery, Carina spied an older couple coming down the street from the other direction. More hungry people hoping for something to fill their bellies. A smoking rafter had crashed down and was bisecting the doorway. She quickly ducked below it and went inside the shop.

"Be careful," Bryce said as he followed her. "I

don't like the look of that ceiling."

Little of the ceiling remained. The passage of the air strike was clearly marked from the roof two floors above, and the clear morning sky lit the bakery's interior.

"Never mind that," Carina replied. "We need to hurry."

The store at the front was already empty. Others had arrived before them to take whatever baked goods had remained on the shelves. The place stank of smoke and burned wood and the air was hazy. Carina walked through to the back of the building.

"Out of my way," a burly man warned, meeting her from the opposite direction. He was carrying a sack of flour over his shoulder.

"Carina," said Bryce in a warning voice.

Carina stepped backward to give him room to pass. "Don't worry, I'm not going to do anything," she said to Bryce. She guessed more sacks of ingredients were stored in the back. If it came down to it, she would do everything in her power so that her family didn't starve, including fighting, but things weren't so bad that she'd been forced to challenge someone else for their food, yet.

When the man had passed her by, Carina stepped into the backroom of the bakery. The Sherrerrs' attack hadn't penetrated there and the power in the city had been off for days, so the place was dark.

She could hear scuffling, and she paused a moment so her eyes could adjust to the low light. A few seconds later Carina saw the source of the noise: two figures were grappling over something.

One of the figures was gripping a small sack to her chest and the other, also a woman, was trying to pry it from her fingers. Carina guessed the sack contained salt or a similar precious substance.

Bryce had gone past, his hands outstretched to feel his way in the dark. "Here! Here's something. Carina, come and help me lift it."

"Let go," one of the fighting women exclaimed. "I saw it first. It's mine."

"You might have *seen* it first," her opponent replied, "but I *took* it first. Go and look for some more yourself if you want it that bad." She released her hold on the bag to grabbed the other woman's hair, wrenching her head down. Screeching, the assaulted woman punched the other in the face. The bag dropped to the ground, spilling its contents. Both women wailed with dismay, dropped to their knees, and began to fight over who would scoop the spilled material back into the bag.

Carina quickly strode past the scene and joined Bryce, who was twisting the neck of a large sack in his hands, preparing to pick it up.

"Are you sure you can carry it?" Carina asked, eyeing the size of the bag.

"I'm going to try."

Bryce's frame had been coltish when Carina first met him, probably due to the disease he'd been suffering, but since he'd been cured he'd put on muscle. Carina guessed he was now stronger than her so she let him take the lead. But as he heaved the sack upward she helped by gripping the sides and lifting.

"Let's go," Bryce panted. He marched toward

the front of the bakery, his back bent under the weight of the flour.

Carina hoped they would make it back to their latest hideout. She would take a turn in carrying the sack. And if they couldn't manage it, they could always tip some of the flour out somewhere hidden and return for it later. Pleased with their find, she followed Bryce into the front of the bakery.

The older couple she'd seen in the street a few minutes previously was now barring the store exit. The man and woman were dressed in clothes that had once been fine but were now grimy and torn. The pair stood in intimidating silence, their intent clear from their glares.

Bryce had halted, his knuckles white from the strain of holding the heavy sack.

"Hand it over," said the man. "Then you can go." His arms were folded over his chest in an attempt to look intimidating.

Carina felt a trace of pity for the couple. Though Ostillon had only been at war for a short time the residents were already showing signs of starvation. Formerly well-off, they were clearly unused to surviving in difficult circumstances.

"There's plenty more back there," Carina said, gesturing behind her. "We don't have to fight over this."

"I don't believe you," said the older woman. "How do we know you haven't taken the last one? This is the first place we've found that hasn't already been ransacked floor to roof."

Bryce dropped the sack. "Here, take it. We can get another one."

"No," said Carina. "They can get their own." She

walked up to the couple. "Move out of our way. We aren't a charity. Stop wasting our time. I told you there's more inside. Go and look for yourselves."

When the man and woman still didn't budge, Carina grabbed one of their shoulders each and pulled the pair forward, out of the doorway. The woman stumbled.

"Hey," the man exclaimed, raising a fist, "how dare you—"

Carina deflected his blow and punched his jaw. She hit him hard enough to make him stagger but not black out.

Wisely, the man heeded the warning. Rather than fight back, he went to his wife's side and hurled insults at Carina.

She helped Bryce as he lifted the sack onto his back. They stepped out into the street.

"Why did you have to hit him?" asked Bryce. "They were old, and there was plenty to go around."

"That wasn't the point. If those two are going to survive, they need to learn to pick their fights. We're obviously younger and stronger than them. If they aren't careful they'll die quicker than by starvation. Things on Ostillon are going to get a lot worse before they get better. I hope I taught them a lesson."

"So what you're saying is," Bryce said with a wry smile, "you manhandled that woman and punched that guy for their own good?"

"Something like that."

Carina and Bryce were walking briskly and looking around them. Now that they'd finally found something to eat, they had to make it across the city to their latest refuge without losing their precious find to another looter.

As always, Carina was carrying a metal canister of elixir, but she could only use the liquid to Cast as a last resort. Castiel was undoubtedly scouring the war-torn planet for his mage siblings. He would be on the watch for news of strange, inexplicable occurrences, like things moving without being touched or people disappearing into thin air.

The problem of what to do about her Dark Mage sibling had plagued Carina ever since she'd agreed with Parthenia that she had to do *something*. All she'd accomplished so far was to keep her family out of his clutches. That, and provide them with food and a safe place to sleep. She would have to be content with the fact they had survived another day.

The puzzle of how to deal with Castiel would have to wait a while.

CHAPTER TWO

"What is it?" Darius asked, jumping up onto his toes and bouncing when Carina and Bryce carried the sack between them downstairs into the basement. "What did you find?"

"Some kind of flour," Carina replied, dropping her end of the heavy sack. Her back was sore and her hands were aching and raw from gripping the rough material. Every day she and Bryce had to walk farther to find food. Looters were steadily cleaning out the city. Carina wondered if the time had come to relocate somewhere else on Ostillon.

"Is that all?" Darius asked. He'd opened the sack, revealing the grainy white powder. He looked up at Carina, his big brown eyes plaintive.

"What do you mean, is that all?" asked Bryce. "We can make some delicious fried cakes from this stuff."

"Except we don't have any oil or fat," Oriana said.

"Baked cakes, then," Bryce replied.

Oriana pouted and rested her chin on her hand. She was sitting next to her twin on a broken-down sofa that had been dumped in the basement of the abandoned, partially demolished house.

Parthenia was playing a card game with Nahla on the dusty rug, using cards made from plaspaper trash. She put down her cards, stood up, and walked to the sack. "This looks great. Very fresh. Thanks, Carina and Bryce, for finding it for us. I guess it's still pretty dangerous out there." She looked pointedly at Oriana, who muttered, "Thanks, Carina and Bryce."

Darius murmured something unintelligible and returned to the cards.

"I'll make us something to eat," Parthenia said. "You two sit down and rest."

Carina could have hugged her sister. Of her four mage siblings, Parthenia was the only one who wasn't showing the effects of their luxurious, privileged upbringing. Though initially Darius, Oriana, and Ferne had risen to the challenges of a harder life than they were used to, the novelty had clearly worn off. Parthenia was the only one who hadn't complained even once.

Carina struggled to pity the others. They might have fallen from the highest to the lowest tier of society, but they were only leading the same life Carina had lived for six years after Nai Nai had died. Hunger, cold, and danger were daily obstacles to be faced. She hated to admit it, but she was disappointed in them.

"I'm going to rinse off," said Bryce. Flour from the sack had coated his neck and hair.

"Let's start a fire," Carina said to Parthenia.

"There's no need. I can do it myself."

"I know you can. I only want to help." Carina dragged the sack of flour across the basement floor to the cooking area.

In one corner of the basement at the back of the house, a window opened high on the wall. Parthenia had made a small hearth from closely stacked stones on the concrete floor. Carina was pleased to see that a stack of wood had appeared nearby. Parthenia must have sent the children to gather it while she and Bryce had been gone. Now that the power in the city was out, fire was their only source of warmth and heat for cooking. And of course, naked flames were essential for making elixir.

The wood was very dry and looked like it came from an item of furniture. Dry wood was essential to avoid creating smoke that would choke them in the small room and, worse, alert others to their presence.

Parthenia scooped out a couple of cups of flour into a bowl and stirred in water until the flour clumped into crumbs. Then she clenched together the crumbs to make a ball and began to knead it.

"You look like you know what you're doing," said Carina.

"I would watch our chef in the kitchen sometimes, when Father wasn't home. Cooking looked like fun. I didn't think I would ever have the chance to do it, though. Father would have had a fit if I'd told him I wanted to do something as demeaning as create dishes for others."

Carina picked up a frying pan they had taken from another abandoned home days previously and brushed the dust from it. Oriana was correct in saying they had no fat for frying, but perhaps if they were careful the flour cakes wouldn't stick. She piled pieces of wood in the hearth and then balanced an iron grid on the stone wall so that it sat over the sticks.

Bryce returned, his hair wet. He invited Nahla and Darius to play cards and sat down with them.

"It's a shame there's no Cast for cooking," Parthenia said. She pulled a piece of dough from her ball and began to flatten it into a disc.

Carina said, "I used to think that too when I had no home. I can understand that it isn't possible to create food from nothing, but why we can't transform raw ingredients into cooked, I don't know. If there is a Cast for that, Nai Nai never let on. She always cooked everything from scratch. Maybe cooking is too complex. Casting seems to only cover simple actions, like Locate, Send, Transport...and Fire."

She lifted her elixir canister and took a sip of the liquid. The Fire Cast was one of the first Nai Nai had taught her. She concentrated for a moment and wrote the character in her mind. When she opened her eyes, the wood in the hearth was already smoking. A moment later a flame licked up and quickly the rest of the sticks caught alight.

Parthenia put the frying pan on the iron grid and after the pan had warmed for a few moments, she put a circle of uncooked dough into it.

Parthenia's expression was closed and somber. Carina wondered what she was thinking. Parthenia had spent so much of her life hiding her true feelings out of fear of angering her father, neutral features were a habit.

Carina put a hand on her sister's shoulder. "Thanks for all your help. We couldn't do this without you."

The response Carina received was unexpected.

"Do what, exactly?" Parthenia said tightly as she broke off a second piece of dough and began to roll it between the palms of her hands.

"You know what I mean," said Carina. "You've helped us to stay safe and survive."

"Oh, thanks." Parthenia's tone was hard and her eyes had turned stony. She picked up a stick to push under the flat flour cake in the frying pan to flip it.

"Parthenia, what's wrong?"

Her sister glanced over her shoulder at Bryce, Nahla, and Darius, playing cards on the rug, and Oriana and Ferne, who were dozing on the sofa. She said softly, "When are we going to do something about Castiel? We have to find him. We have to stop him."

Carina sat back on her haunches. "So that's what's been bothering you? You know we can't Locate Castiel. Unless we have something personal of his, we can't do it. He could be anywhere on Ostillon, or he might even have left the planet now."

"But he's probably still at Langley's estate. We could look there. Carina, you've seen what he's doing. We can't let him continue."

Carina was only too aware of what Castiel had been doing. Though they hadn't caught sight of their brother, twice they had seen evidence of his activities. Sherrerr forces had managed to break through the Dirksen defenses and land at the spaceport, but the troops running from the landing craft had burst into flames. They had also seen airborne Sherrerr shuttles Split into two pieces and their occupants plummet to their deaths. Unable to find Castiel, Carina and her siblings hadn't been able to Repulse his Casts. They had been forced to watch the scenes helplessly, in dismay.

Castiel had been active in defending Ostillon from the Sherrerr attack, and Carina guessed that he'd only begun to explore the range of devastation he could inflict on the Dirksens' enemies.

"I know," Carina answered her sister. "I know we should do something. I just don't know how to stop him. We can't go to Langley's estate, assuming he's still living there. We would be captured the minute we came anywhere near the place. It's too risky. And I don't have any other ideas."

In truth, Carina knew she had not put serious effort into catching Castiel. She doubted she could manage it alone, yet she feared for the lives and freedom of her siblings if they helped her. The war between the Sherrerrs and the Dirksens wasn't her fault or her problem. Why should she risk her family by trying to put an end to Castiel's attacks?

Another worry niggled at her: what would she do with Castiel if she succeeded in capturing him? Could she kill her half-brother in cold blood, cruel and evil as he was? She'd killed enough people to last her a lifetime. And if she couldn't kill Castiel, what then? How could she keep him confined for the rest of his life?

"Oh no," Parthenia exclaimed. Smoke was oozing from the cooking flour cake. Parthenia tried to push the cake out of the pan with the stick, but it was stuck.

"Dammit," Carina said. She grabbed the pan but the handle was hot. Wincing, she pulled down her sleeve and tried again. This time she removed the frying pan from the grid and put it down on the floor.

"Is the food ready yet?" Darius called out.

Parthenia leaned forward to poke the burnt cake with her stick, trying to remove it from the pan. But as she did so the bowl of dough on her lap fell off and landed upside down. She gave a groan and lifted the bowl. The dough was dirty and ruined.

"It's okay," said Carina. "We can make some more."

Parthenia rose to her feet to scoop more flour out of the sack.

Suddenly, an explosion roared above. The basement shuddered. Parthenia was thrown to the floor.

Nahla and Darius were screaming, but Carina couldn't hear a thing. Bryce stared upward, his mouth hanging open. Carina followed his gaze. A crack was splitting the ceiling apart. Grainy dust rained down into her eyes.

"Get under the sofa," Carina yelled at the kids. Her voice sounded distant and faint.

Parthenia was trying to stand. Carina launched herself at her sister, forcing her down. She covered Parthenia with her body. Bryce dove over

Darius and Nahla.

Something heavy and solid crashed into the back of Carina's head. She knew no more.

CHAPTER THREE

Carina could smell grass. It seemed so long since she had smelled that green scent. She inhaled deeply, savoring the aroma. Warm air was bathing her. She heard insects chirping.

She opened her eyes. She was on her back, and above her a pale blue sky stretched wide. Tall stalks of wild grass surrounded her, motionless in the still air. A scratching sound was coming from her right-hand side. Carina turned her head. Only a few centimeters from her nose, a long-legged insect crouched on a grass blade and rubbed its serrated limbs together.

Someone grabbed her shirt and tugged at her, turning her over. Agony flared up from her thigh. Carina yelled out in pain. She was back in the basement. Dust was choking her, her ears rang, and above her the sky was aflame.

Bryce's face appeared in her view. "Carina, are you okay?" She could barely hear him but she could read his lips. How long had she been out? It felt like only a few moments. He was lifting chunks of rubble away from her.

"I'm okay," she replied. She tried to move, but excruciating pain lanced from her leg again. "I think my leg's broken."

Carina felt movement below her. She remembered she was lying on Parthenia. Her sister was trying to get up.

"Find the elixir, Bryce," said Carina. "Bring it to me." He disappeared from her view. Carina tried to move off her sister but the slightest motion sent nauseating waves of pain. "Darius! Nahla!" Carina gasped, fighting nausea from the pain. "Where are you?" She couldn't see anything except the remains of the basement ceiling. Jagged edges lined the break. Through the gap she saw red and orange clouds, reflecting fire. A smoky haze blew across the sky.

Parthenia twisted and Carina cried out as her leg jerked. The broken ends of her bones ground against each other. "Please, stay still," she said to her sister. Perhaps Parthenia answered but Carina didn't hear.

Bryce was back and Carina felt faint with relief. He was holding the familiar canister. He unscrewed the lid and put a hand behind her head, lifting her to take a sip. Carina swallowed the elixir and shut her eyes. The pain made it hard to concentrate. She had to focus.

Carina imagined herself pushing the pain from her leg down into a box, closing the lid, and locking it. A sense of calm arrived. Carina wrote Heal and Cast the character out, willing it downward to her broken bone.

She exhaled, long and slow. Gingerly, she reached her mind out to her leg. The pain was gone.

Carina found her hearing was also returning. She could hear a hum growing louder, filling her ears. It wasn't a hum. It was a roar. The roar of flames. Had the Sherrerrs bombed the city with incendiary devices? Or had the clan attempted another landing, and Castiel had Cast Fire on the city?

Parthenia moved beneath her again. Carina shifted off her sister and took the elixir canister from Bryce. Parthenia crawled out from rubble and plaster dust.

"Are you all right?" Carina asked her.

Parthenia nodded.

The remains of the basement lay around them. The sack of flour had been exploded by a block of masonry. The sofa was in pieces. The window had shattered into thousands of pieces.

"Where are the others?" Carina asked Bryce.

"They're okay. They're outside already. I took them upstairs and came back for you. We have to get out of this area. Now."

"But we need to bring the elixir," said Parthenia.

"It's all gone," Bryce replied. "The container was crushed. We only have what's left in the canister."

"It's okay," said Carina. "We can make more."

They stepped over the rubble-strewn floor to the staircase and climbed stairs choked with debris from the destroyed house. At the top of the stairs the rest of the children were grouped in a huddle anxiously waiting. Their clothes and exposed skin were blackened with smoke.

"Where to now?" Bryce asked when they reached the top.

Carina didn't know. Burning buildings surrounded them. As her gaze lit upon one it collapsed, sending sparks shooting into the sky and red-hot bricks scattering across the street. Carina scanned three hundred and sixty degrees. Every avenue seemed to be blocked. A man flew from a doorway, screaming, on fire. Carina grabbed the two younger children's heads and buried their faces in her stomach. The man hurtled down the road as if trying to escape the flames that were consuming him.

"We have to Transport," she said. "If we try to walk out of here..." She didn't need to say more.

"But where can we go?" Oriana wailed. "We don't know anywhere that's safe anymore."

"Nowhere is safe for certain," said Parthenia. "But we can get away from the city. We can go somewhere unpopulated that won't be of interest to the Sherrerrs." She held Darius' shoulders and turned him around. "Do you remember the forest we were in when we first came to Ostillon? Do you think you can Transport us all there?"

The little boy's face was pale and his eyes were wide with fear, but he nodded.

"Are you sure it's safe, Parthenia?" Carina asked. "How far away is this place?"

"I don't know exactly. It's on this continent. I think Darius can do it."

"Not all of us at once, though" said Carina. "It's too risky. Two at a time, in case something goes wrong. And let's swap personal things so we can find each other again if we're separated."

They hastily emptied pockets and found small items to share around. Darius had a pair of dice that he split between Parthenia and Oriana. Nahla gave Carina a hair ribbon. Bryce had nothing except a ring. He pulled it from his finger and pushed it into Carina's open hand, folding her fingers over it. In ten or fifteen seconds they were done.

The buildings around were going up like torches. The air was growing unbearably hot and Carina was struggling to breathe. She handed Darius the canister.

"Who goes first?" he asked.

"Bryce, Ferne, and Nahla together."

"No," said Oriana. "I want to stay with Ferne."

"I want Bryce to be with Nahla," said Carina.

"I can do it," Darius said. "Nahla is only little, like me."

Oriana pouted, but she hugged her twin goodbye.

"Transport those three first," Carina told Darius, "then Oriana and Parthenia, and then you and me."

Carina had a lot of faith in her little brother's mage power, but fear he would fail clutched at her. He was young and he was frightened, which would make it more difficult for him to Cast.

"Do I Transport everyone to outside the ranger's tower?" he asked Parthenia.

"No, that's too dangerous," she answered. "He might still be there. He could see us appear from nowhere. Aim for somewhere half a kilometer away, out in the wild country beyond the tower. But not in the forest."

"Okay." Darius sipped elixir and closed his eyes. In another couple of seconds, Bryce, Ferne, and Nahla were gone.

"Hurry up and Transport me," Oriana said. "I don't want to lose Ferne."

A crack split the air, and with a rumbling crash a wall collapsed a few meters behind them. Burning masonry tumbled toward them.

"Watch out," Carina cried. Grabbing Darius' arm she dragged him away. Parthenia and Oriana crowded close. The roaring of the flames was growing louder.

"Please hurry, Darius," Oriana begged.

He lifted the canister again and took another sip. How much elixir was left? Carina didn't know. She hoped none of the liquid had slopped out when she'd pulled Darius away from the collapsing wall.

Parthenia and Oriana disappeared.

"Is there enough left for both of us?" Carina asked.

Darius shook the canister. "I think so."

"Okay. When you're ready."

Her little brother tipped up the canister and swallowed the remains of the elixir. He closed his eyes. Concentration creased his brow.

"Just don't put me in mud," said Carina.

A small smile lit Darius' face, and Carina gripped his hand.

They Transported.

CHAPTER FOUR

Castiel watched the shuttle's display in silence. The Dirksen pilot was flying closer to the Sherrerr flagship, *Nightfall*. True to her name, the massive vessel was dark against the stars, carrying no external lighting.

The ship had hung in the Floria planetary system for days, like a brooding overlord, while the Sherrerrs launched their deadly attacks on Ostillon's military installations, manufacturing and transportation hubs, and major cities. For days, no Dirksen military spacecraft had broken through the ship's defenses. Many had been destroyed in the attempt.

As Castiel watched, more Dirksen military vessels were harrying *Nightfall* in an effort to distract its crew from the small, unarmed shuttle.

Dirksen reinforcements were on their way to the Floria system, but if nothing turned the tide in the battle for Ostillon by the time they arrived the planet would be smoking ash and rubble.

Castiel recalled a Sherrerr attack on another Dirksen planet, Cestrath, a military stronghold. His half-sister, Carina, had destroyed an ocean side military base there. In that attack the Sherrerrs had wanted to preserve as much of the planet's infrastructure as they could, and they'd succeeded. The capture of Cestrarth had yielded valuable equipment and intel, and the planet was now a Sherrerr stronghold.

His father's clan clearly had no intention of treating Ostillon in the same manner. Their attack had been relentless and devastating. Did the Sherrerrs know that the world harbored the mages who had escaped them? The moment that Carina had taken the mages from *Nightfall* the Sherrerrs had lost key, highly effective resources. If the clan thought retrieval of them would be impossible, it made sense to attempt to destroy the mages instead.

Mages made excellent weapons, as the Sherrerrs aboard *Nightfall* were about to discover.

"Are you within range to do your thing yet?" Reyes Dirksen asked. "I don't think we can get much closer without attracting their attention."

"Don't speak to me," said Castiel. "I have to concentrate." Ignoring Langley Dirksen's son sitting next to him, he filled a beaker with elixir. He'd been watching the battle, noting the position of *Nightfall's* weapons when they fired. He regretted he hadn't asked his father for a tour of the ship during the weeks he'd lived aboard it. If he'd known where the fuel tanks were situated he could have Cast Fire into them, the same as his brothers and sisters had when they destroyed the

Dirksen shipyard.

Langley Dirksen had warned him that capturing the ship was preferable to destroying it. Such a vessel would be a valuable asset for the Dirksens. Nonetheless, Castiel itched to make a spectacular end to *Nightfall*. That would make the clan take notice of him. His standing among them would rise to heady heights. As it was, his contribution to Ostillon's defense had been all but ignored, it seemed. He knew he could do so much more and rise so much higher, if only they would let him.

Another of his problems lay in the fact that more than half of his long-distance Casts failed. He hadn't had the same practice as his siblings, and though he'd watched many of the lessons their mother had taught, the information she'd passed on had been patchy and unreliable. Carina had demonstrated what a properly trained mage could do.

"I really think you should do something now," urged Reyes.

"And I said, be quiet!" Castiel snapped. He hated Langley's son. Langley had insisted that Reyes must be his constant companion, as if he were a child who needed a chaperone. Yet Reyes was only three years older than himself. Langley was attempting to control and keep tabs on him, but she was overstepping the mark.

Langley Dirksen was one of several problems Castiel intended to solve when he had the opportunity, when he had helped to rid Ostillon of the Sherrerrs' presence and showed the Dirksens that a new force had appeared in their midst.

Castiel lifted the beaker to his lips and

swallowed its contents in several large gulps. He'd practised the Cast he intended to make many times with success, but he'd never attempted it on such a scale before. He could not use Split again. Though his strength and skill grew stronger every day, he could not tear such an immense vessel as *Nightfall* in two. Also, despite his annoyance, he had heeded Langley's exhortation to avoid damaging the ship if he could.

What he intended would not be spectacular, but it would be effective. The remaining Dirksen fleet would be able to move in and complete *Nightfall's* defeat.

Castiel closed his eyes, centered his consciousness, and dove deep into his mind, just as his mother had taught his siblings. In his mind's eye, he wrote the character, Break. Next, he copied it several times. Finally, he propelled the characters at the Sherrerr flagship, aiming them according to his memory of *Nightfall's* weapons. Break was a simple Cast that required little strength but sending the characters across the void exhausted him.

"Have you done it yet?" Reyes voice intruded.

"Dammit," Castiel yelled, leaping to his feet. His flailing arm knocked over the jug of elixir and it clattered on the floor, the liquid spilling out in a flood. He leaned his face into Reyes' and said softly, "If you speak to me again while I'm Casting, I'll rip you apart."

Reyes' eyes became hooded and his expression sullen. If Castiel's warning scared him, he didn't show it. Castiel threw himself into his seat and rubbed his temple. He muttered, "It's done."

The shuttle pilot had diplomatically ignored the altercation. He said, "The Sherrerr ship has stopped firing."

Castiel returned his attention to the display. What the pilot had said wasn't strictly true. One of *Nightfall's* pulse weapons continued to operate, but his Cast had taken out most of its offensive capabilities. Relief and delight mingled in his chest. His Casting ability was improving. He doubted Carina could have done any better.

The Dirksen ships were not slow to take advantage of *Nightfall's* weakness. They were drawing closer to the ship and concentrating their fire on the remaining weapons.

"You did it," said Reyes, though his tone was not celebratory.

Was Reyes jealous? Castiel didn't particularly care. If Langley Dirksen's son envied his ability, the fact meant nothing to him. Except for one thing: though the Dirksens as a group might relish the fact that they had a mage working for them, the Dirksens as individuals might be less happy about the situation. Castiel imagined that politics and power struggles within the clan could yet impede his progress.

His sudden appearance and rise to prominence could arouse suspicion and envy among its members. With the exception of Langley, the Dirksens might deeply distrust anyone who carried the name Sherrerr, no matter how many times Castiel demonstrated his loyalty.

Then there was the natural resentment that mage abilities excited in people. Castiel was all too aware of this. He had felt the same way himself for many years. He guessed that some of the Dirksens would like nothing better than to put an end to this upstart intruder, even at the clan's expense. He was certain that this was how Reyes felt, and especially so. Langley Dirksen's son had once been the focus of his mother's attention, but now that attention was directed at Castiel.

"They're boarding her," the pilot exclaimed.

Castiel couldn't see any Dirksen ships next to *Nightfall* on the shuttle's display. He had removed his comm in order to concentrate on Casting, so he slid the device into his ear. One of the Dirksen vessels had indeed successfully gained entry to *Nightfall*. The boarders would be fighting the ship's crew in the passageways, trying to gain control of the ship.

"Retreating to a safe distance," said the pilot.

"Why?" Castiel asked.

"I'm guessing the Sherrerrs might not want us to have their ship," said Reyes.

"You got it," the pilot said.

Acceleration forced Castiel forward as the shuttle swept away from *Nightfall*. Dirksen ships were taking out the weapon that his Cast had failed to break. Other Sherrerr ships continued to try to defend the flagship, but the Dirksens were successfully fending them off.

The battle for Ostillon was turning, and Castiel's contribution to the fight had been instrumental, the key success. No Dirksen could deny it.

In return, Castiel would demand recognition. He wanted a seat at the Dirksen war council. His own dwelling and compensation were to be expected, but what he wanted and needed was control.

Without power within the clan his position could become precarious.

As the shuttle sped from the scene of the battle, Castiel closely watched the result of his work unfold. A second Dirksen ship gained access to *Nightfall*. The ship's final working weapon ceased firing. A shuttle departed from the second boarding Dirksen ship, possibly transporting Sherrerr captives to Ostillon.

Nightfall hung in silence in the glittering black, Dirksen vessels surrounding it. Brilliant streaks of pulse fire cut across space as the remaining Sherrerr ships fought to save their captain.

Castiel wished he knew a Cast that would allow him to see inside of things. He greatly desired to watch the close combat of the Sherrerr and Dirksen forces in *Nightfall*. He wanted to see the exchanges of fire, the hand-to-hand combat, and the blood. He wanted to hear the screams. But that was all denied to him. Was there such a See Cast? He didn't know if it didn't exist or if Mother had kept it secret.

He recalled that brat, Darius, claiming he had invented a new Cast once. If it was true, the first thing he would do when he captured his brother would be to force him to create more Casts. Was Darius on Ostillon? Castiel hoped so. He hoped that, along with his other siblings, Darius had not been able to escape. Things were soon to become more stable, and then Castiel would be able to initiate a thorough search for his brothers and sisters.

As long as they were free they would be a threat to him. He needed to have them under his control, as well as benefit from their power.

Castiel heard that a third Dirksen ship had latched onto *Nightfall*. The flagship was truly defeated.

The pilot suddenly cursed, breaking Castiel's train of thought. He looked up at the display. *Nightfall's* dark hull was rent with radiant light. She was blasting apart.

"Are we safe?" Reyes asked.

"Still working on it," came the pilot's stiff reply.

Rather than allow their flagship to fall into Dirksen hands, the Sherrerr command had given the order to self-destruct. As Castiel watched, *Nightfall's* hulking form dissolved into a snowstorm of speeding, flashing debris.

It was the beginning of the end of the Sherrerrs, and the start of Castiel's journey to power.

CHAPTER FIVE

"When we settle down somewhere," said Parthenia as she scraped fine wood shavings from a stick with a knife, "the first thing I'm going to do is brew enough elixir to fill a water tank."

Carina smiled. She was squatting next to her sister, waiting for her to finish adding elixir ingredients to the metal canister. It was good to hear Parthenia talk about the future lives they would lead and not harp on about catching Castiel. Perhaps she'd given up on the idea.

A gust of cold wind blew, cutting through Carina's clothing and raising goosebumps on her skin.

"Hurry up, Parthenia," Oriana said. "It's freezing here and I'm starving. Even if we manage to catch anything it's going to take ages to cook it."

Darius had done exactly as Parthenia had asked him and Transported them to the wild lands on the other side of the continent, near where he and his sister had first arrived on Ostillon. His effort had used up the last of their elixir.

It was a bleak wilderness. Aside from the tall tower in the distance where, according to Parthenia, a ranger called Jace lived, the area was empty of human habitations. The reason was obvious: the land was poorly drained and swampy. On higher ground beyond the tower a dark, dense forest grew.

They were safe for the moment, that was clear. But the downside of uninhabited regions was that they contained little to support human life. There was no fresh, clean water, nothing to eat, and nowhere to shelter. If they hadn't had the ability to Cast, they wouldn't have lasted longer than a few days. As it was, survival was still difficult.

After long searching, Carina had managed to find a firestone. Bryce had discovered an old bird's nest that would serve for tinder in a thicket, and the children had gathered whatever dry wood they could find. The water had come from one of the many pools in the area. Though it wasn't clear, let alone clean, boiling the water would make it safe to drink. They also had Carina's canister in which to brew the elixir. When Parthenia had added all the ingredients, Carina would make a fire.

But she remained worried about their long-term prospects. They had been hiding from Dirksen patrols and Sherrerr attacks for nearly a week, struggling to find enough to eat and to stay warm and dry. Carina felt they had been skirting the edge of a drain, managing to avoid being sucked down for now, but how much longer could they keep it up?

"It's ready," Parthenia said, putting down

Carina's knife.

"Good job," said Carina. "Okay, everyone. Gather around. I want you to watch me."

"But we've watched you do that before," said Nahla.

"I know," Carina replied. "And as soon as we have plenty of materials and time, I'm going to make you all practice until you can do this yourselves. You never know, one day you might not have me around."

Darius grabbed Carina around her neck. "You're always going to be around."

"I hope so," she said. "But you're going to watch me carefully anyway, right?"

Darius replied, "Uh huh," and sat on his haunches, staring so intently at the little pile of tinder Carina almost laughed.

"Oh, hurry up," said Oriana. "I'm so hungry."

Carina struck the knife against the firestone, causing sparks to fly onto the tinder. Before long smoke began to ooze from the dry material. Carina teased a glow by blowing steadily into its center. When a flame licked up, she put the tinder into the little pile of sticks and knelt on the ground so she could blow into the pile. She added thicker sticks when more flames sprang up. Soon, the metal canister was sitting at the edge of a small fire, its contents simmering.

"Are you sure there are things we can eat in there?" Ferne asked Parthenia as they waited for the elixir to be ready. He was referring to the forest at the top of the ridge about half a kilometer away.

"There are *things*," his sister replied. "I'm

guessing we can eat them."

"Providing we can catch them," Oriana said, her hand absently resting on her stomach.

"This should help," said Carina. The elixir had simmered long enough. She lifted the hot canister away from the embers so that the liquid could cool.

With sufficient time, Carina guessed that she might be able to make a trap to catch a forest-dwelling animal, but she'd had an idea that might be quicker and less reliant on woodcraft.

"Bryce," she said, "I'd feel better if you stayed here with the younger children. Do you mind? You could make us a shelter to sleep in tonight while I'm gone."

He looked at the forest and then the sun, which was entering the lower quarter of the sky. "Are you sure you're going to be okay in there by yourself?"

"If Parthenia and Darius spent hours walking through it alone without incident, maybe that means nothing dangerous lives there. But I wasn't planning on going by myself. I wanted to take Ferne with me."

"Cool," said Ferne. "I'd love to come."

"Can I come too?" Oriana asked.

"No," replied Carina. "I only need one of you in case I catch something heavy." She wanted to encourage her sister to be more independent and less clingy with her brother. For all Carina knew, the two could be separated at some point. Oriana was old enough to survive alone, if she didn't pine for Ferne.

"Okay," said Bryce. "I already found a dryish spot about four hundred meters that way." He pointed in the opposite direction to the forest.

"When you come back, look for us over there."

"We will," said Carina as she pulled her shirt sleeve over her hand again to pick up the canister and screw on the lid. The elixir would cool some more on the way to the forest.

"Be careful climbing that ridge," said Parthenia. "It's slippery."

"Come on," Carina said to Ferne, who happily jumped up and joined Carina's side as she began to walk toward the forest.

"What are we going to do after we catch Castiel?" Ferne asked when they'd been walking for a few minutes.

"What do you mean? Are you asking what we're going to do with him or where we'll go next?"

"Both, I guess."

"Honestly, Ferne, I'm not happy about taking you all with me to help capture Castiel. I know I agreed with Parthenia that he's too dangerous to be left to his own devices, but I'm having second thoughts about involving you guys too. The Sherrerrs and the Dirksens won't stop at anything to get him back, or to capture any of you. I've been wondering if I should take you all away and try to put as much distance between ourselves and Castiel, and the entire galactic sector as possible."

"Maybe we should kill him," Ferne said quietly. He was looking away from Carina as he spoke.

"I don't know if I could do that," Carina said. And if anyone was going to do it, it had to be her. She couldn't expect any of Castiel's siblings to murder their brother, no matter what he'd done. Their mother had already killed their father. That was enough trauma for a lifetime.

***

A ditch sat at the bottom of the ridge where the forest grew. They slid down the bank into the lower area and Carina found herself up to her knees in mud. This stuff was slimy and evil-smelling too. Ferne, being lighter, hadn't sunk in so deeply. He helped Carina to free her legs from the clinging suction. They crossed the ditch and began to climb the bank.

The canister of elixir had cooled until it was only warm. Carina slipped the container into her shirt so she had both hands free to scale the steep slope.

Ferne climbed beside her. At one point, his grip on a tree root slipped and he slithered down a short distance. Carina waited for him to climb up to her level.

"I used to think it would be nice not to have to live in our big house with Father," Ferne said as he toiled upward, panting. "I wanted to go to school like other kids and play outside in parks and in the streets."

"You might still be able to do that, one day."

Ferne reached Carina, and they continued to climb together. The top of the ridge and the outskirts of the forest lay a few meters higher.

"I know this must sound funny," said Ferne, "but sometimes I almost wish I was back in our house in Ithiya."

"I think it's natural to feel like that. Your life was a lot easier then. Living out in the real world is hard." Carina guessed Ferne also missed his mother, though he didn't say it. Wishing Ma was alive again would mean wishing the woman continued to remember her life of enslavement and torture, the murder of the man she loved, and everything else she'd endured. She'd suffered enough and had been glad to let go. Ma was better off where she'd gone, wherever that was, though Carina missed her too.

Carina reached upward, grabbed clumps of grass, and pulled herself up onto the level surface. She turned around and held out a hand to help her brother up. Then they walked quickly into the trees. Behind them, the sun was already lowering to the horizon. It was a good time of day to be catching animals. The ones who were around during the daytime would be going to their sleeping spots and the nocturnal beasts would be waking up and moving around.

But they had a long evening ahead of them. Assuming they could catch something, they still had to carry their catch down the ridge, cross the odorous ditch, climb out of it, and then find the rest of their party in the darkness. Casting Transport would be a temptation but they couldn't waste precious elixir on doing things they could do themselves.

Carina searched for animal tracks in the failing light. If she could find a well-used trail, it would make her task easier. She didn't find one before the evening grew too dark to see well, but they did walk into an area of open ground among the trees. Carina looked for a branch low on a tree, and said to Ferne, "This one's good. Let's climb up."

"You're planning on catching a bird?" Ferne asked.

"I'm planning on catching whatever happens

by."

"Oh, I get it," her brother replied.

They climbed about four meters up into the tree and stopped at a branch that overlooked the open ground and would bear their weight. Now it was only a matter of waiting and watching.

Carina had heard that an animal's sense of smell was stronger than a human's, and she worried that any wild creature that came near would detect their scent and be frightened away. She needed the animal to stick around long enough for her to Cast. She hoped the stench from the mud in the ditch would cover their smell.

Ferne shifted close to her, causing the leaves in the tree to rustle. She put her arm around her brother and they benefited from their mutual warmth as they waited. Night fell and the air grew colder. Forest noises started up in the stillness—distant nocturnal bird calls, shuffling and scraping in the undergrowth, and the calls of frogs—but Carina saw nothing she could Cast upon.

Carina became stiff and her muscles ached. She knew Ferne must feel worse than her after the soft life he'd led, yet he remained stoic.

Finally, their patience was rewarded. Ferne must have heard the noise first, for Carina felt him stiffen a moment before she also registered the sound of an animal walking close by. She held her breath and hoped the beast would enter the open patch of ground. In anticipation, and to avoid spooking the creature by her movement, she removed the lid from her canister and lifted the container to her lips, all the while never taking her eyes from the gap in the tree's leaves where she could see the forest floor, barely visible in the darkness.

A four-legged animal stepped daintily into the spot. Its limbs were slim and delicate. An elegant neck rose from its body and led up to a head that tapered to a fine nose. Small horns sprouted next to each of the creature's ears. The animal was so beautiful, Carina hesitated to take the next step, but she had a family to feed.

She drank a mouthful of elixir and closed her eyes, keeping the image and location of the animal clear in her mind. She Cast Enthrall. When she opened her eyes, the creature had disappeared. Had her Cast missed?

Ferne began to climb down the tree.

"Where are you going?" Carina asked.

"You got it. It moved away but then it stopped. I can see it from here."

Carina also dropped to the branch below and then the next until she reached the ground. Ferne had already reached the creature. It was standing still, alive but motionless. If Carina had been able to communicate with it she could have instructed the animal to do whatever she wanted now that it was Enthralled. But she didn't want to do that.

She quickly pushed the animal down onto its side and then knelt on its neck. "You probably want to look away," she said to Ferne. As her brother turned around, Carina grabbed the animal's head and twisted it hard, breaking the creature's neck.

Dinner for that day was arranged. But what kind of life would the following days bring for them all? How long could they survive as they had been, hunters and hunted? Carina decided she needed to talk with her siblings that night. They could not continue to live on Ostillon.

CHAPTER SIX

Carina licked her fingers and then wiped them on her pants, noticing how grubby the material looked even in the poor light from the campfire.

The animal she'd killed in the forest had filled everyone's bellies, according to the looks of satisfaction on her siblings' and Bryce's faces. It was the first time since the Sherrerrs had launched their attack they had all had plenty to eat.

"This is a good shelter you built while Ferne and I were gone," she said. With help from the children, Bryce had slung a long, straight branch between two small trees and then piled many more branches against it before covering the lean-to in dead plant material. The open side of the construction faced the fire and the ground beneath it was piled with more dead grass and ferns.

"It is, isn't it?" said Parthenia. "If you can find more animals for us to eat, we can live here for days. Now that we have elixir a fire won't be a problem. We only have to remember to keep our supply topped up so we don't run out again."

Darius and Nahla were already asleep, curled up like family pets next to the fire. Everyone else was looking sleepy too, but it seemed to Carina this was a good time to tell the others her decision.

She took a breath, knowing that Parthenia wasn't going to like what she was about to hear. "Actually, I was thinking it was time we moved on."

"You mean we should go back to the capital?" Parthenia asked. "I guess so. We aren't likely to find Castiel around here. But—"

"No, I mean we should leave Ostillon. I think I need to face up to the fact that it's too dangerous for you all here with Castiel around. I need to take you somewhere safe. Then maybe I'll return to deal with him?"

"But we don't have time for that," Parthenia said. "We have to stop him now. He plans on taking over the Dirksen clan. When he's in control of everything he'll be untouchable, and who knows what horrible, evil things he'll do? Imagine if Father had ever run the Sherrerrs. He would have treated everyone the same way he treated Mother. It would have been hell."

"I understand what you're saying," Carina replied. "But is any of that your fault? The Sherrerrs turned a blind eye to how your father treated Ma, and the Dirksens worked hard to get their own mage. Well, now they have one. They'll reap what they sowed."

"I'm not talking about the Sherrerrs and Dirksens, I'm talking about the ordinary people. If

Castiel gets any real power, they'll suffer terribly."

"She's right," said Bryce. "With Castiel running the show, it's going to be a bloodbath."

Carina thought back to her childhood and the cruelty she'd endured at the hands of the 'ordinary people.' She thought about the number of times she'd been beaten and tortured by non-mages. She had spent most of her short life viewing regular folk as a threat, yet she also hadn't forgotten the help she'd received from Bryce and from the military on the *Nightfall* when she'd escaped with her family.

Carina's shoulders sagged and she nodded. "You're right. I have to prevent Castiel from doing his worst. But not here or now. You are all my responsibility, and we're barely surviving day to day. When I know you're safe I'll find Castiel and try to stop him."

"Do we get any say in this?" Parthenia asked.

"We'll go outsystem," said Carina, ignoring her sister. "We'll find somewhere quiet and off the trade routes. When you're settled I'll hunt for Castiel and remove him from the scene." Carina remained unsure of exactly what the latter entailed, but she would cross that bridge when she came to it.

"How can we leave Ostillon?" asked Ferne, chewing on a bone. "We don't have a ship."

"No," Carina replied, "but maybe we can get one, especially now that everything's in disarray due to the war."

"Can you fly it too?" Bryce asked.

"I should be able to figure it out. I flew the Sherrerr shuttle, remember?"

Oriana said, "But where can we go? How do we know what planets are safe?"

"I'll figure that out too. The first thing we need to do is find ourselves a ship."

"You've sure got a lot of figuring out to do," said Bryce.

***

Later on, Carina and Bryce were lying face to face inside the lean-to. Everyone was asleep except for them. Bryce had his back to the fire and Carina faced him. Darius lay behind her and the rest of the children occupied the remaining space.

"Are you sure about leaving Ostillon?" Bryce asked Carina softly.

She forced open her closing eyelids. "I'm sure. I know we need to do something about Castiel, but we're too weak right now. When I was a merc I learned the hard way what happens when your enemy outclasses you. Our company owner put us in hard-to-win situations more than once. That woman has blood on her hands. I'm not going to make the same mistake with my family. I hate Castiel and fear what he might do, but going in weak and unprepared isn't going to work. We could all end up dead."

"Okay, I hear you."

They looked into each other's eyes for a few moments without speaking. Carina recalled the first time she'd met Bryce. It had been months previously, when she'd been at the end of her hope of finding another mage. Bryce had followed her home while she was in a drunken haze.

They'd kissed. In all the time they'd spent together since then they'd never been so close again. He'd helped her aboard the Sherrerr flagship, nearly at the cost of his own life, and he'd searched for her on Ostillon for days. He'd said he wanted to be with her. But could a relationship between a mage and non-mage ever work out? Would Bryce be able to resist the desire to control her for his own gain?

Carina didn't know. She couldn't deny that he had proven his loyalty and trustworthiness several times over, but how long would that last? She feared becoming closer to him, knowing that her feelings would make her vulnerable.

"Good night," she whispered.

"Good night."

Long after Bryce fell asleep, Carina also began to drift off.

She was on a plain of tall grasses and wildflowers. A young, strong sun was scorching her exposed skin. The buzzing of insects filled her ears. Carina knew she'd been in that place before but she couldn't remember when. Distant voices sounded behind her, and when she turned around she saw some people approaching, wading through the grass as if walking through a shallow sea.

She didn't think she could have imagined a more dissimilar group of people. One of them was very old and swathed in robes, barely hobbling along and using a stick for support. Another was tall and broad with a beard that reached to his middle. A third wasn't much more than a child, about Parthenia's age, Carina guessed.

As she was watching the group, the oldest lifted her head and looked directly at Carina. She raised a hand in greeting, and for some reason Carina felt compelled to return the salute.

But before she could lift her hand, something drew her back to Ostillon.

Carina opened her eyes and immediately knew what had wakened her. Footsteps. They were drawing closer. The walker was doing his or her best to be silent, but the ground was littered with plant matter the children had dropped while gathering material to construct the shelter.

From her position next to Bryce, Carina could see only the night sky. She lifted her head a little to peer over her sleeping companion. The fire had died down but the embers glowed, making it difficult to see much, but she could make out a tall, black figure ten or twelve meters away from their camp, moving slowly toward them.

Carina had prepared for exactly such an event. Darius was sleeping against her back. She had told him what he had to do. She only hoped that grogginess from being woken from a deep sleep wouldn't affect his Casts.

She reached behind her, groped for her brother's shoulder, and sharply shook it.

"Darius, wake up," she muttered. With relief she felt her brother stir. "Someone's coming. Remember what I said? Do it now."

Despite his young age, Darius quickly and silently responded to her request. Carina was proud of how fast her little brother had learned to react quickly in dangerous situations. Proud but also sad. She hoped he would be able to lead a more normal childhood one day.

He was moving, feeling for the elixir canister

she'd given him. Carina fixed her eyes on the approaching dark stranger. Who was he? Was he the ranger that Parthenia had mentioned? She guessed the man must have spotted the glow of their fire. She'd thought they weren't in sight of his tower.

Was there nowhere on Ostillon where they could safely hide?

No. They had to escape the planet, providing this stranger didn't catch them first.

Suddenly, Bryce was gone. Darius had made his first Cast. Bryce, Nahla, and Oriana would have an abrupt awakening after their Transport. No one now lay between Carina and the stranger.

The shadowy figure was at the fire. Carina heard Ferne or Parthenia stir, probably awoken by the abrupt disappearance of their sleeping companions. Then their movements turned to silence as Darius Transported them from the place.

The strange, large man stepped forward. He was standing above Carina, looking down into her open eyes. He was black-haired and his face was wreathed in a thick, black beard.

Hurry up, Darius!

"No! Wait," the man exclaimed.

He disappeared along with the fire, the swampy wood, and the darkness.

CHAPTER SEVEN

The shuttle that had carried Castiel and Reyes from the space battle was landing, and Castiel's excitement was mounting at the thought of the reception he was about to receive. Would Sable Dirksen be waiting at the spaceport to congratulate him? Or perhaps he would be conveyed to her residence for a private audience. After all, it might be too much to expect the head of the Dirksen clan to travel out to meet him, in spite of the significant service he had performed in striking a monumental blow against the Sherrerrs.

The pilot gave the signal that it was safe to disembark. Castiel immediately rose from his seat and almost collided with Reyes.

"I should be first onto the ramp, don't you think?" Castiel asked the lanky Dirksen.

"Why? What difference does it make?"

Castiel only gave him a knowing smirk in response. Langley's son had to be brimming with jealousy over Castiel's achievements. It was no surprise, but Reyes couldn't hope to live up to Castiel's abilities. He had better accept it for his own peace of mind. Not that Castiel cared.

After pushing Reyes aside, Castiel strode the short distance to the shuttle's ramp. It was dark outside though dawn was approaching. The lights at the capital's domestic spaceport were not shining, no doubt as a safety measure. Castiel peered into the darkness, seeking in vain for the figures he expected to see. He'd thought Langley would be there at the very least to express her praise for his success.

But look as hard as he could, Castiel could see nothing except the dark shape of a hover vehicle near the end of the ramp.

Reyes took his turn to push Castiel out of the way before walking toward the vehicle. "What were you expecting? A welcoming committee?" he sneered. "They don't care who you are. You're only a tool to them."

Castiel hesitated, shocked at the unexpectedly lackluster response to his achievement. He had destroyed the Sherrerr flagship, for stars' sake. Or, rather, the Sherrerrs had destroyed it themselves, but he had incapacitated the vessel and turned the tide of the battle. He could hardly believe that no one had been sent out to congratulate him.

Ire simmering in his breast, Castiel stomped after Reyes. Langley's son was likely to leave without him if he wasn't quick. He climbed into the hover vehicle and then sat in furious silence as they were whisked from the spaceport.

From the corner of his eye he could see the amused look on Reyes' face. An urge to punch the expression away rose up in Castiel. What would Langley do if he hit her son? What *could* she do? He had plenty of elixir. He would be able to inflict a lot of damage on her and other Dirksens before he ran out.

But what then? He didn't have enough elixir to kill them all, and he didn't want to. The clan was useful to him. Their networks of people, supplies, and military power spanned the regions under their control in the galactic sector. It would take him years to build a similar infrastructure. It made more sense to use the one that was already available.

Castiel purposely relaxed his clenched fists, recalling that his father had rarely reacted in haste. He should follow his parent's example. The Dirksens were clearly too stupid to grasp his true worth. Demonstrating their error to them would take time. He had to be patient, and he had to concentrate his efforts on giving them explicit examples of his power. He had to impress them and, perhaps even more importantly, he had to intimidate them. Fear brought respect.

Father had controlled his family through fear. If it hadn't been for that bitch Carina, he would have raised the family's status to the top of the Sherrerr clan. Castiel wanted to follow his father's lead and succeed where he had failed, albeit in a rival clan.

When they arrived at Langley's mansion, the woman was waiting at the door, dressed in a shimmering gown. Castiel climbed out of their vehicle and walked to the entrance. Langley embraced Reyes first, Castiel was not slow to note. Then she hugged him, but he didn't move his arms from his sides and remained stiff-backed.

Langley's jubilant expression faltered and she looked a little afraid, presumably as she realized what she'd done wrong. "Come in, come in. I took the liberty of arranging a victory celebration. I hope you don't mind. You must be tired. Would you like to freshen up and change before joining us?"

Somewhat mollified, Castiel replied, "No, it's fine. I can go straight in." So the Dirksens had organized a reception for him after all. Perhaps Castiel would not need to provide them with a potent demonstration of his abilities.

Reyes asked to be excused from attending the party, saying that he was tired and would go to bed. Castiel guessed that he hated the prospect of seeing someone else steal the limelight.

Reyes left them in the hall and Castiel went with Langley to her entertaining room. As he stepped through the open double doors, he scanned the space to see who was present to offer their congratulations. Dark displeasure settled over him again. Only seven or eight people were there, and Castiel had met them all previously at Langley's soirees. They were minor figures in the Dirksen clan.

He figured that the head of the military division would probably be too busy to make the event, but where was Sable Dirksen? Didn't she realize what he'd done for her clan?

Langley was watching him nervously. "Why don't you come in and sit down? You must be exhausted. What would you like to drink?"

"You're right," said Castiel. "I am exhausted. I changed my mind. I think I'll retire for the evening." Without another glance at the assembled inconsequential Dirksens and hangers-on, Castiel spun around and left the room.

He strode to the staircase and climbed the steps two at a time. When he reached his room, he unlocked the door and marched inside, slamming the door closed. He carefully locked it. He had insisted on a new lock and that he held the only key to it. As the only mage the Dirksens had, he couldn't be too careful.

Castiel paced the room, fuming. Who the hell did the Dirksens think they were? Did they really imagine that he would put up with their neglect and slights?

He halted, realizing he mustn't allow their rudeness and stupidity to get to him. He didn't want to do anything rash and jeopardize his current position, unfairly low though it was. Castiel sat down on his bed and pulled off his shoes as he considered his next step.

He returned to his earlier plan of giving a clear, intimidating demonstration of what he could do. There had to be something that would make the Dirksens sit up and take notice of him. They had to understand that he wasn't some insignificant foot soldier who could perform convenient tricks for them.

Castiel picked up his interface and logged into the news network. Castiel scanned the information. It was sparse. The news of the defeat of the *Nightfall* had only just begun to filter through to the media.

He was curious about the fallout from the flagship's destruction, wondering how he could exploit the event. The Dirksen ships and crews that had been boarding the Sherrerr flagship had all been destroyed, but the remainder of the Sherrerr fleet had withdrawn from the field of battle. It looked like Ostillon was saved, for the time being.

Anger rose up in Castiel's belly again. *He* had saved Ostillon, and the Dirksens had rewarded him with a lukewarm party with nobodies.

The news updated and the new information caught his attention. Several prisoners had been taken from the Sherrerr ship before it self-destructed. Castiel wondered who they might be. Father had introduced him to several of the higher-ranking officers. They had clearly been uninterested in him at the time and only condescending to his father, but that didn't matter. This could be the opportunity he was looking for.

Castiel didn't know what the Dirksen interrogation methods were, but he was confident he could Cast something that would be more effective. Spectacularly effective, in fact.

When Sable Dirksen saw what he could do, she was guaranteed to show him the respect he deserved.

CHAPTER EIGHT

Dawn was arriving at the spaceport. Darius had Transported Carina and the others to another remembered spot on Ostillon: outside the spaceport fence. It was the place where Ferne had almost died from a Dirksen crossbow bolt.

Reyes Dirksen's star racer had sparked a fire in the forested area, but the undergrowth was beginning to grow back. Rain had fallen recently. The early morning air was chilly and humid and the new, young forest vegetation was sodden.

Carina crouched at the fence, surveying the take-off and landing zones and the hangars. Descending through the clouds high above was a shuttle coming in to land. The place had been taken over by Dirksen military, no doubt due to their own spaceport's destruction. The presence of military vessels was a big impediment to Carina's plans. Stealing a military craft would be way more difficult than sneaking onto a civilian vessel and ejecting the pilot.

The problem with Casting was the lag. A round fired from a gun was immensely faster than the operation of a Cast. Even slipping a knife under someone's ribs was quicker. That was the reason Stefan Sherrerr had been able to control his mage wife and children. It also meant the ability to Cast wasn't a sure-fire guarantee they could steal a ship.

After her inadequate amount of sleep, Carina eyes and head were sore with tiredness. In the remains of the forest behind her, the children waited. Unable to lie down due to the wet ground, they were complaining about being cold and exhausted. But Carina didn't want to waste time resting before they made their attempt to leave Ostillon. They were back in dangerous territory, where Sherrerrs could launch another attack or Castiel might find them.

The incident at their campsite in the uninhabited wild lands had made their danger even clearer. If someone could find them there in the wilderness, nowhere on Ostillon was safe. They had to leave at the earliest opportunity.

A hand on her shoulder jolted Carina from her ruminations. Bryce was beside her, his features drawn with tiredness. Carina guessed she looked the same. Trying to survive the last few days had taken its toll on everyone.

"What do you think?" Bryce asked, nodding at the shuttle that was lowering to the ground a couple hundred meters away.

"No, not that one. An incoming vessel is likely to be low on fuel. What we want is one about to take off, refilled with enough fuel to take us a reasonable distance. Then we have to hope there's another system within shuttle range. I don't remember noticing one on the map when we were on our way here after escaping the *Nightfall*. Then we have to pray we aren't shot to pieces trying to navigate through a battlefield." She gave Bryce a tight smile.

"But if we try to steal a shuttle that's about to depart, won't troops be on their way over to it?"

"Yeah, probably." Carina's lips drew to a line. "This isn't going to be easy." She stood up, her leg muscles stiff with squatting for too long in the damp weeds, and walked over to her brothers and sisters. They were huddled in a group under the blackened limbs of a dead tree. Darius was writing numbers in the dirt with a stick, and the others were sitting on their haunches, listless, pale, and sleepy-eyed. Only Parthenia was active, replenishing their small supply of elixir over a smoky fire.

That was another reason they had to act quickly. It was only a matter of time until someone at the spaceport became curious about the line of smoke reaching up into the sky, now clearly visible in the growing light of the approaching sun.

"Listen, everyone," Carina said. "I need your help. I need ideas on how we can work together to steal a ship and get off this planet. We have to cross the open space of the landing and take-off zone, get aboard a ship, and fly it out of here. And we have to do all of that without being shot. I've run a few scenarios through my head, like Casting Fire on a building to create a distraction or Transporting troops a safe distance away, but everything seems too risky. I don't know if a fire will distract everyone, and even if we managed to Transport every soldier out of that place, more could arrive in shuttles from the battle any minute."

"Instead of Transporting the soldiers away," said Ferne, "could we Transport their weapons to us? Then we can fight them."

Carina smiled. "You think we can take on all the troops in that place?"

"We can try," Ferne replied.

Parthenia suddenly rose to her feet. "Whatever you all decide to do, you can count me out. I'm staying here. You can take all the elixir. I'll make some more for myself when you're gone."

"What?!" Carina exclaimed. "No! No way, Parthenia. You have to come with us. If you stay here alone you'll die. Or, even worse, Castiel will catch you."

"I won't leave this planet while he's still a danger," said Parthenia. "I just won't do it, and you can't make me. You've decided for all of us, without even a discussion about it. Who made you the leader? I don't have to do whatever you say just because you're the oldest."

"I'm not trying to boss you around," Carina retorted. "I'm trying to save your life, you idiot." As soon as she'd spoken, Carina regretted her words. She knew she shouldn't have been so blunt, but she was running on a couple of hours' sleep and she was worried out of her mind about how she was going to protect everyone.

But the damage was done. Parthenia strode away into the darkness.

"Dammit."

Carina walked after her sister. "I'm sorry, Parthenia. I shouldn't have said that. Please, come back. Don't go off by yourself. It's dangerous around here."

"Leave me alone," Parthenia yelled. "Go and steal your spaceship. If I have to stay here and stop Castiel by myself that's what I'll do."

"No." Carina had caught up to Parthenia. She grabbed her arm. Parthenia halted and faced her.

Carina said, "I can't let you do something so stupid. If you take on Castiel alone he'll catch you and keep you captive. He'll torture you until you do whatever he says. Do you want to end up like Ma?"

"Then help me, Carina. Don't run away. We'll never be this close to him again. If we leave now we'll lose our best chance."

Carina tried to think of a way to make her sister understand how wrong she was. Parthenia still saw Castiel not as a highly dangerous Dark Mage but as her brother and so her responsibility. She was only fifteen and had no perspective on the situation. Carina was three years plus a lifetime of hardship older than her.

She made another attempt to make her sister see reason. "Look. I promise I won't give up on trying to stop Castiel. I'll come back. I only—"

"That's what you said before." Parthenia's eyes were hard, glittering in the rays of the rising sun.

"What? When?"

"When Castiel was holding me at Langley Dirksen's mansion. You tried to rescue me, but then when things got tough you left. You said you would come back, but you didn't. I had to get away from him myself."

Carina was momentarily lost for words. What Parthenia was saying was true. Faced with the surprise Repulse Casts from Castiel, Carina had been forced to leave her sister in his clutches. She'd intended to return with a military-style assault, but then the Sherrerrs had begun their attack.

Carina grabbed her sister's shoulders. "But I hadn't abandoned you. You saw me fighting in that mech battle, right? I was trying to win enough money to buy weapons. I was coming back for you. I just didn't get a chance. I would never have left you with Castiel, Parthenia. Not while I had breath in my body. Please believe me."

Parthenia's defiant expression wavered. She broke eye contact. "It doesn't matter now. I'm staying here. Take the others somewhere safe and then come back and help me deal with Castiel, if that's what you really want. You can use the elixir canister to Locate me when you return. I've touched it often enough."

Carina was about to speak, but then she changed her mind. She could tell her sister had passed the point where she could be reasoned with. It was no surprise. They were all at the end of their tether. But that meant more than anything that they had to get away, and soon, before fatigue and stress caused one of them to make a fatal error.

"Okay," said Carina. "If your mind's made up."

"It is."

Carina gave her sister a brief hug before turning

and walking back to the group. Not for a second would she entertain the idea of leaving Parthenia behind on Ostillon.

CHAPTER NINE

"Where's Parthenia?" Darius asked as soon as Carina returned from speaking with her sister.

Her little brother had drawn numbers all over the damp dirt under the dead tree, and he'd managed to transfer plenty of dirt onto his face too. His voice trembled. The little boy was on edge, only just holding himself together. Guiltily, Carina reminded herself of his sensitivity to the emotions of people around him. They were all suffering their individual fears and worries, but Darius was suffering his and everyone else's too. No wonder he seemed to spend every spare moment obsessively writing numbers. He was probably trying to distract himself from the extreme feelings that resonated inside him.

"She's gone for a walk," Carina replied.

"But she is coming with us, right?" asked Oriana.

"Yes, she is."

"Phew," Ferne said. "Thank the stars for that.

I'd hate to leave her behind."

At the spaceport a military shuttle was taking off, carrying troops to Dirksen ships defending the planet. They needed to leave too, and soon.

"We aren't leaving Parthenia behind," said Carina. "I'm going to go and get her. Give me the elixir, Oriana."

The girl reflexively lifted the canister, but then she paused. "Why? What are you planning to do with it?"

Glances passed between the siblings. The possible reasons Carina would need elixir to bring their sister back were very few.

"Just give it to me," Carina snapped, and held out her hand.

Oriana moved the canister close to her chest. "If you're planning what I think you're planning, I don't think you should do that."

Carina reached out and snatched the container from her sister's grasp. "I didn't ask your opinion." She marched into the forest again, pacing quickly to return to Parthenia before she lost her under the trees.

When she spotted her sister's figure moving among the blackened tree trunks, she called her name, adding, "Wait a second."

Carina was gratified to see Parthenia pause, and she sped up her pace.

"What do you want?" asked Parthenia. "Did you change your mind? Are you staying to help me with Castiel after all?"

"I just want to give you something," Carina replied, stalling for time.

"What?" Parthenia's features scrunched into a

squint as she peered at Carina, noticing she was holding something behind her back.

Carina was close enough. Even if Parthenia ran, she wouldn't have time to run out of sight. Carina removed the canister lid and sipped elixir.

"What are you doing?" Parthenia asked. Then realization dawned. "No! How could you? How could you do that to me?" She backed away. She turned and began to run.

Carina Cast, and her sister's footsteps slowed to an amble.

"Parthenia, come here."

Carina's sister reversed her direction and returned to Carina. The guilt she'd felt when she remembered Darius' ultra-sensitivity to others' emotions was nothing compared to the remorse and shame that swept through her now. When Parthenia drew close enough to see her eyes in the weak morning light it was clear that, inside, she was fighting Carina's instruction with all the will she could muster. Sadly for her, no one possessed the strength of will to defy a fresh Enthrall Cast. However, the fury and fire in Parthenia's gaze indicated that Carina would have to watch her carefully.

"Let's go back to the others," said Carina.

Her siblings had obviously been discussing what she might be doing while she was away. They watched in silence as Carina and Parthenia walked up.

"Oh, Carina," Oriana breathed, watching Parthenia's slow, dragging steps. "What have you done?"

Darius threw down his stick, hugged himself,

and began rocking as if he was in terrible pain.

"I've done what I had to do," Carina replied.

There was an unwritten rule among mages that you never Cast Enthrall on another mage against their will. Practising on each other while learning the Cast was fine, but it could only be with the other person's consent. Taking away another person's control of themselves was only acceptable if the mage was in danger or if you were trying to save them from harm. A mage would have to be doing something truly terrible to justify another mage Casting Enthrall against them for any other reason. Parthenia had only wanted to exercise her free will.

"Has anyone had any ideas on how we can steal a shuttle?" Carina asked, keeping an eye on Parthenia.

"But, Carina…." said Ferne, his tone soft and distraught.

"I said has anyone had any ideas on how we can steal a shuttle?" Carina repeated forcefully. "I'm guessing we have enough elixir for about ten Casts. That should do it, but which ones should we use? Bryce? Do you have a plan?" Carina felt about to fall apart. Shame and guilt over breaching her sister's trust were killing her. Would Parthenia ever forgive her for what she'd done? Perhaps not, but Carina was also certain she would Enthrall her sister again in a heartbeat. If Parthenia hated her for the rest of her life that was okay. At least this way she might live.

Darius murmured something too quietly for Carina to catch. "What did you say?" Carina asked, touching his shoulder. Darius flinched and looked up at her suspiciously.

Had she lost his love too? Carina bit her lip. "Darius, if you've thought of a way we can get out of here, please, tell me."

"I can Cloak us," he replied. "Or, I think I can. But we have to stay close together."

Of course. After everything that had happened since the Dirksen patrol ship had boarded the stolen Sherrerr shuttle, Carina had forgotten the Cast her brother seemed to have invented.

"So no one else will see us cross the spaceport?" she asked. "We won't be seen entering the ship?"

"I don't think so. I don't know for sure. I only ever did it on myself before, except when we were running away from Father's clan." Darius winced like pain was wracking him.

"Okay, let's try it," Carina said. And the sooner the better. If Parthenia was especially strong-willed—and Carina was guessing she was—the Enthrall Cast wouldn't last long. Carina would be forced to use more elixir to Cast again, and again, until she had gotten her sister so far from Ostillon she wouldn't be able to return.

***

Bryce, Ferne, Oriana, and Darius were on the other side of the fence, waiting.

"Parthenia, climb the fence," Carina repeated. At her first command, Parthenia's limbs had moved but then they had frozen. The Cast and Parthenia's willpower were battling within her. Carina could hardly believe the Cast was losing influence so quickly. Her sister's inner strength was powerful, and she was clearly also raging inside.

"Climb the fence!" Carina yelled.

Parthenia jerked forward like an automaton. She raised her hands and gripped the wires, her features twisting.

Darius pressed his hands against his face and turned away.

Parthenia began to climb. Carina kept pace with her. "Oriana, make sure you have the elixir ready to hand to me as soon as I reach you." She fixed her gaze on Parthenia, fearing to see her other sister's reaction to the instruction.

Barely able to restrain her impatience, Carina watched Parthenia climb over the top of the fence. As she climbed down the other side, Carina followed her, hoping Parthenia would remain under the control of the Enthrall Cast all the way onto the shuttle.

Carina jumped the last couple of meters of fence.

"Are you ready, Darius?" she asked.

"I don't know." He moved his hands away from his face. Tears had mixed with the dirt, creating wet grime that lined the depressions of his eyes and lips.

"What do you mean you don't know?" Carina glanced toward the spaceport. If they were going to act, they had to be quick.

"I can't think. It hurts too much."

"You're hurt?" Then Carina understood. "You mean it hurts inside?"

Darius gave two quick nods.

Carina knelt on the wet ground and hugged her little brother. "I'm sorry. I'm so sorry we're all hurting you. But can you please try? I'll hold you if it helps."

"Okay." Darius' voice was quiet. "I'll try."

"Oriana," Carina said.

Her sister handed her the elixir and Carina held the canister's open mouth to Darius' lips. The boy took two large swallows before closing his eyes. Carina held him as she imagined Ma would have done, gently and comfortingly. The poor kid. He'd been through too much, and now the fate of all of them rested on his shoulders. But she had no choice except to ask this of him if he and his siblings were to be safe.

"It's done," Darius whispered.

"It is?" Nothing seemed any different. Carina wasn't sure what she'd been expecting but she'd been expecting *something*. "Are you sure we're Cloaked? Is there a way we can tell?"

"When I played hide-and-go-seek I could always see myself. I only knew it was working when no one could see me."

Great. Darius appeared to have invented a Cast that threw a barrier of invisibility over objects, rather than making the things themselves invisible. "Okay, everyone. It's time to go."

Parthenia's eyes blazed.

"You too, sis," said Carina. "Sorry, but this is how it has to be." She gripped the elixir canister tightly as they set off across the shuttle landing area. "Bryce, can you watch for any vessels coming in to land?"

"Oh, don't worry. I already thought of that," he replied, his gaze turned upward.

If Darius' Cast had worked and they were not visible, an incoming shuttle could land right on top of them. The Cloak Cast had made the Sherrerr shuttle they had used to escape undetectable to scanning equipment.

They were fast-walking in a huddle. Carina had maneuvered Parthenia so that she was in the middle and Carina stuck close to her side.

In the distance a line of troops appeared and began a slow jog across the landing ground. Everyone except Parthenia drew a collective breath. If the Cast hadn't worked and they could see the soldiers, that had to mean the soldiers would see them. But none of the men or women reacted. There was an audible sigh as they understood that they were Cloaked.

Carina checked the direction the troops were traveling and followed the line with her gaze. She found herself looking at a military shuttle that had seen better days. But despite the vessel's decrepit appearance, it was definitely where the soldiers were headed. Engineers were swapping out fuel rods.

"That's our flight over there," said Carina. She grabbed Parthenia's upper arm. "Run, everyone, but stick together so you don't move outside Darius' Cast. If we don't want a big fight we have to reach that ship before its passengers do."

The mage family broke into a run. Carina could feel Parthenia's resistance in her bicep. The muscle was cramping in Carina's grip. She could also hear a low groaning or growling sound. Carina looked around, trying to see where the noise was coming from. Then she realized it originated in her sister. Parthenia was trying to speak.

Just another few minutes. Please.

Carina doubted any guards would have been

posted at the vessel, but she guessed there might be personnel inside. The pilot would be there for sure, waiting to ferry the approaching detachment of troops to the battle.

Carina checked the speed of the soldiers who were running toward the shuttle. She estimated her little group would arrive first, but not by much. They would have to close the doors fast, but what to do with the pilot? They couldn't take him or her along.

A sudden alteration in the running soldiers' attitude caught Carina's attention. They were staring directly at them! No. Not all of them. Only Ferne, who was in the front. He must have run too far ahead.

"Ferne, slow up," Carina called.

Her brother eased his pace, but the damage had been done. "Hey! What the hell do you…? Huh? Where'd he go?" The troop leader turned to his subordinates as if to confirm he hadn't been seeing things. The men and women looked just as confused as him.

The pause allowed Carina and her family to reach the shuttle first with time to spare. She ran up the ramp without braking, forcing Parthenia onward. Inside, two privates were lounging on the seats. They froze in surprise, mouths and eyes wide. Carina realized she must have run outside Darius' cloak.

The other mages and Bryce burst into the cabin. Carina saw everyone except Darius. She would have to trust he remained Cloaked.

Thanking the stars they only had two Dirksen soldiers to fight, Carina went for one, leaving the other to Bryce. She grabbed the shocked woman's weapon from her grasp, hauled her to her feet, and forced the muzzle into her back. Pushing the woman in front of her, Carina compelled her to leave the shuttle. Bryce's target followed soon after. As soon as the two soldiers set foot off the ramp, Carina told them to run or feel the heat of the shuttle's engines as she took off.

When Carina returned to the cabin, the pilot had conveniently appeared.

"Please do the honors," Carina said to Bryce as she pushed past the pilot to reach the flight controls. "Darius, Cloak the ship, as soon as you can."

Her gaze roved the displays and interfaces. Thankfully, the old-style, basic vessel had the equivalent old-style basic controls.

"Pilot's gone," Bryce yelled from behind her. Carina closed the doors. Now she only had to—

"Parthenia, no!" someone yelled. Carina recognized Ferne's voice.

The sound of fighting was coming from behind her. *Dammit.* Parthenia was already shaking off the Enthrall Cast. Carina jumped up and ran into the cabin.

Bryce was trying to hold on to Parthenia but she was fighting like a wild thing trying to grab the manual override for the doors. Carina couldn't risk her sister trying to escape while they were taking off. She ran up to Parthenia and punched her in the jaw. Her sister's eyes rolled back and she fell limp in Bryce's arms.

The dull sound of rounds being fired into the hull was coming from outside. Assuming Darius had Cloaked the shuttle, the soldiers were firing blind at the place they had last seen it.

If Carina had wanted to send an unmistakable message to Castiel about the location of his mage brothers and sisters she could not have done a better job.

She ran back to the pilot's seat and started up the vessel's engines. The only safe option left was to leave Ostillon. Carina flew the shuttle into the morning sky.

CHAPTER TEN

It had taken an escalating series of threats the following day, culminating in the ultimatum that Castiel would abandon the Dirksens entirely and set out on his own, before by late evening Langley finally agreed to forward his request for an audience with Sable Dirksen. Reyes' bug-eyed mother had let down her facade and displayed real anger and rancor for the first time in Castiel's experience. He guessed that she wasn't as important in the clan as she liked to make out, and that she'd intended to use him to raise herself, claiming credit for all that he did.

The assent from the head of the Dirksens arrived. Confident that Sable Dirksen was clearly curious to meet him, Castiel was soon on his way to an unknown destination. Langley's servants did not transport him. He had waited to be picked up, and when the hover car arrived, it was unmarked.

He gazed out the window of the vehicle, trying to track where he was going. The driver had lifted the vehicle a couple hundred meters above ground level, and they were traveling fast. Castiel lost all sense of where he was. The driver hadn't spoken a word to him yet, and Castiel doubted very much that she would tell him where they were going.

The long journey should have been tiring, especially considering he hadn't slept since defeating the *Nightfall,* but Castiel found he was alert with anticipation. He congratulated himself on making exactly the correct move. Who did Langley Dirksen think she was, denying him his right to shine? Who was she to make herself his 'manager'?

Castiel looked down at his clothes. Though Langley had supplied him with new suits, he worried that his appearance wasn't fine enough for the company he expected to meet soon. Father had —quite rightly—always been particular about such things. The problem couldn't be remedied. His clothes would have to do. He planned on impressing the leading Dirksens in other ways.

A mountain range in the distance was looming closer and seemed to be the place the driver was heading toward. Castiel peered ahead at the white peaks reflecting the moonlight. Sable Dirksen certainly seemed to prefer living in remote places. It was no surprise that the Sherrerrs hadn't discovered her base and destroyed it.

A realization hit, and Castiel's stomach muscles tightened. The privilege of access to the head of the clan carried a heavy price. As soon as he knew her secret location, his life would be forever under threat. If Castiel did not live up to whatever expectation Sable Dirksen had of him, she might decide his existence was a risk she wasn't prepared to take.

Castiel recalled that the Dirksens had cut Darius' tracer out of him when they held him captive. The clan could be brutal in their methods. Castiel felt for his elixir bottle and took a little comfort in its heavy, reassurance on the seat next to him. It was true the Dirksens could be vicious, but then so could he.

The speeding hover vessel approached the mountains at an incredible pace. Soon they were swooping through a narrow pass. A face of a slope was rapidly approaching, dead ahead, but the driver wasn't turning the vehicle. Was she having some kind of seizure?

"Hey!" Castiel shouted. But it was too late. He threw up his arms. They were going to fly right into solid rock and be smashed to pieces on the mountainside.

But instead of hitting the slope, the vehicle passed through it and they emerged inside a brightly lit natural cavern. Disbelieving what had happened, Castiel looked over his shoulder and saw a rock wall. The slope must have been some kind of hologram. The pilot braked heavily, throwing Castiel forward. Then they were rapidly lowering to the cave floor.

The driver still did not speak a single word. The soft hum of the engine ceased and the door next to Castiel opened. As he stepped out he saw three similar hover vehicles and a fast-looking, immaculate shuttle also docked in the cavern. Ahead of him, two doors pulled apart. The message was clear.

Castiel set off toward the open doorway, his finger hooked through a circle in the elixir canister, trepidation creeping up on him. But he had made his bid and he had won. Now he had to see it through to its conclusion.

"Please come this way," said a man.

From his clothes, Castiel judged the man to be a servant. Castiel didn't deign to speak to him but followed the man through rough-hewn passageways. The floor was worn smooth and though the walls were rough, in some places they were shiny, as if people had rubbed against them for centuries. Along the corners of the passage long, carved decorations ran where the walls met the ceiling. Most of the carvings were of animals Castiel did not recognize.

He had the impression that the place had been inhabited for hundreds or thousands of years, but he didn't think it was Dirksens who had lived there. According to what Langley had told him, the clan had only inhabited the planet in substantial numbers for a few years.

They arrived at a set of doors that stood twice as high as Castiel. The servant said something into a panel, and the doors split apart.

This was it. He was about to meet the person who wielded the ultimate power in the Dirksen clan. Castiel breathed in deeply and stepped through the opening. A stone chair stood alone directly ahead of him on the far side of the large chamber. But the chair was empty. Puzzled, Castiel looked around the hall.

"I'm over here," said a voice.

Castiel's eyes widened when he saw the voice's

owner. A young woman who looked not much older than himself sat in a luxuriously padded armchair at the far end of the room. Her hair was short and dark, and she was wearing expensive pajamas under a robe. The chair faced a fire of burning logs, at which the young woman was toasting her bare feet.

"It's warmer here," she said. "This place is so fucking cold."

When Castiel hesitated, Sable Dirksen went on. "Well, are you going to speak to me or not? Or did I get up out of my warm, comfortable bed in the middle of the night for nothing?"

Castiel jerked into action, closed his gaping mouth, and walked with what he hoped was a confident swagger to stand in front of the clan leader. Should he bow? Kneel? He hadn't thought this part through.

"My name's Castiel," he said.

"Castiel *Sherrerr*. I know. Langley told me about you. So the old spider has finally given up her prize. You are a prize, right?"

Despite her young years, Sable Dirksen's stare was disarming Castiel.

"I can do things that others can't," he said. Noting Sable's condescending smirk, he added, more strongly, "I am a mage. I helped to defeat the *Nightfall*. I broke its weapons so that it could be boarded." Castiel paused. He was uncomfortably aware that he was falling over himself trying to convince her of his worth. Things weren't going how he'd imagined. He'd imagined performing an impressive feat that would amaze Sable Dirksen, not trying to explain himself like a naughty schoolboy.

"Would you like me to demonstrate?" Castiel asked. Then his nervousness subsided sufficiently for him to remember his original purpose. "I heard some prisoners were taken from the *Nightfall* before it self-destructed. I could interrogate them. Persuade them to tell you everything they know."

Sable's smirk turned into a smile. "You like that kind of thing, do you? I have to admit, when I saw you for the first time just now, I was disappointed. After talking you down for so long to suit her own ends, Langley went to the opposite extreme and talked you up. I guess she wanted me to remember this big favor she was doing me. Yet you don't look like much."

Bitch. How dare she? Castiel fought to keep his expression under control. However, if Sable cared what he thought of her words, she didn't show it.

"But maybe there's more to you than meets the eye," she continued. She raised the back of her hand to her mouth and yawned. "Okay, let's see what you can do." Sliding her bare feet into slippers, she rose from the armchair and walked across the chamber toward an open door in the corner.

Feeling like a lap dog, Castiel followed her. When he had taken over the Dirksen clan, Sable would pay for her words. Walking behind her, he became aware of the movement of her buttocks underneath the rich silken material of her robe. He recalled his father's domination of his mother. Yes, he would pay Sable Dirksen back, in many ways.

***

Sable led Castiel down a set of stairs. The surface

of the walls was smooth, as if cut by machine. He guessed this part of the mountain castle was a Dirksen add-on. They came to a sealed, steel door that slid open as Sable arrived at it. If there was a security mechanism Castiel could not see it. He guessed the door somehow recognized authorized persons.

They stepped into the narrow corridor beyond, where the chill of the cold stone that Sable had mentioned became even more noticeable. More steel doors were set at regular intervals along the passageway. No guards were in place. He scanned the ceiling. All he could discern that was out of the ordinary was a row of black dots. Perhaps they were cameras, or weapons.

"Here we are," Sable announced. Once more, the door opened as she drew near to it. Behind the door stood a transparent wall, and in the cell beyond a woman lay curled on the bare, stone floor. She was nearly naked, and what rags remained on her were blood-stained. Her flesh bore the marks of torture. She was shaking with cold and when she saw them looking in, she shrank into the cell corner. She appeared to sob, though no sound came through the transparent wall.

Despite her state, the woman looked familiar to Castiel. He couldn't remember where he'd seen her on the *Nightfall*. Had she been one of the troops, perhaps? Or was she higher ranking than that? Father hadn't allowed him to walk around the ship very much. Castiel tried to place the woman in his memory.

"Whoops," Sable said. "Wrong one." She backed out of the doorway and gestured for Castiel to leave too, but he had finally recognized the woman's terrified face.

"I know her," he blurted. The prisoner had not been on the *Nightfall* at all, hence his confusion. "She was at one of Langley's parties." Castiel recalled that the woman's hair had been styled into a spiral above her head. That, and the fact that she'd been beautifully dressed the previous time Castiel had encountered her, had added to his confusion.

"Hmm, well spotted," said Sable, adding, "She's a nasty little spy. *Langley's* spy, as you noticed. It'll be a long time before she'll live down her association with the person who revealed our presence on Ostillon to the Sherrerrs."

The cell door closed.

"I'm sure that one has more to tell us," said Sable, "but then I'll take great pleasure in dispatching her. If there's one thing I can't stand, it's disloyalty." She paused and glanced at Castiel before moving to the neighboring door. As it opened, Sable's gaze fell upon him again. Once more, those hard, dark eyes pierced him.

Castiel wondered, if she hated traitors so much, what did she think of him? He was a Sherrerr, yet here he was on the Dirksens' side, offering to help them. Would she ever grow to trust him? But then, he didn't want her trust. He wanted her power.

Castiel looked through the transparent wall of the second cell. This time he immediately recognized the prisoner. *Tremoille.* The Dirksens had gotten themselves a Sherrerr admiral.

Though she was as bloody as the former captive, Tremoille didn't display anywhere near the same terror or submission. Recognition dawned in her eyes as she saw Castiel, but otherwise her features betrayed no emotion.

"You know who you have here, right?" Castiel asked Sable.

"We don't know her name, only her position. Unless she stole someone else's uniform. I'm certain an admiral has a lot to tell us, otherwise I would have had her executed by now. But she's a tough old witch and hasn't revealed a thing."

"She's called Tremoille."

"Thanks. That may be useful to know. Is that all you can do, though? I'd heard you've had some success with affecting spacecraft. I was expecting something more impressive."

Castiel snorted dismissively. "I spent some time aboard the *Nightfall* and I recognize her, that's all." His gaze roved Tremoille's body. The woman had withstood significant abuse. Though he wasn't familiar with the Sherrerrs' military arm, he guessed she had probably been well-trained to withstand interrogation. Employing the regular methods for extracting sensitive information would not produce results. It was the perfect opportunity to demonstrate what he could do as a mage.

Castiel stared into Tremoille's eyes as he considered what to do. What might his father have done in similar circumstances? The answer came, but his method required more than one captive.

"I heard that you had captured a few prisoners from the *Nightfall*," he said.

"We have three," Sable replied. "But this one will do for your demonstration."

"I need two, together."

Sable frowned. "In the same cell?"

"No. One of them has to be able to see her."

"Ah, I think I understand your intention. As it happens, this prisoner has a neighbor." Sable went to the door of the next cell and did something at a panel. Tremoille's cell wall became transparent, revealing a second prisoner from the *Nightfall*. Castiel was interested to see the Dirksens had also captured Calvaley, another high-ranking Sherrerr officer. Calvaley registered his recognition of Castiel with the lifting of his upper lip in disgust.

"Good," said Castiel. "He'll do nicely. He must be able to hear as well as see what's going on."

"Done," said Sable, still at the panel. "And they can both hear us now too."

"Right." Castiel's moment had arrived. He was about to Cast, but then he realized he'd been concentrating on the persuasion part of the interrogation, not on what information Sable wanted him to extract. "What is it that you want to know?" he asked as Sable rejoined him.

"Well, since your family has so kindly destroyed one of our main shipyards, it would be nice if we could return the favor."

Sherrerr shipyard locations would definitely be something that Tremoille and Calvaley would know. "Did you hear that?" Castiel asked Tremoille and Calvaley. "You know what I and my siblings can do. Tell us the shipyard locations, or you'll regret it."

Tremoille spat blood and said, "Fuck off you little c—"

"Shame your sister didn't do the same to you as she did to your father," said Calvaley. "He got what he deserved in the end."

Castiel's hands curled into fists. "My father was worth more than all the rest of the Sherrerrs put together!" It was actually his mother who had killed Father, but he was not about to inform Calvaley of that.

Sable raised a hand to her mouth to cover a smile. Castiel breathed out heavily. *Fuck them.* "Tell us the shipyard coordinates." He waited. "Last chance."

When neither of the Sherrerr officers answered, Castiel was actually pleased. This was going to be enjoyable. He unstoppered his elixir bottle and took a swig. Then he closed his eyes to concentrate. He'd practised the Cast on animals on Langley's estate, with varying results. But the animals had always died eventually, and that was all that mattered.

Castiel wrote the character and sent it out, deciding at the last minute to send it at Tremoille. Calvaley had insulted his father's memory, but Tremoille had called him a nasty word. He wasn't going to stand for that, especially not with Sable Dirksen as a witness. He had to show her that he wouldn't allow anyone to disrespect him.

Tremoille shrieked and clasped her back. She began to wriggle around, as if trying to escape something. But there was no escaping the Split Cast. Calvaley was on his feet and shouting, banging his cell wall with his fists. His words were drowned out by Tremoille's howls of agony.

Castiel was gratified to note Sable's amazement at what was happening. He had finally gotten her full attention. Calvaley was pounding and kicking the wall in fury while Tremoille writhed. A pool of her blood was widening around her. Then, all too soon, it was over.

Calvaley turned his face from the contorted, mangled figure.

"Keep the lights on and their shared wall transparent," Castiel said with as much authority as he could muster. "Let him see her for the rest of the night. Then in the morning we can ask him for the coordinates again."

Sable pulled her gaze from Tremoille's remains. "Come out here." She closed Tremoille's cell door.

"That was dumb," she said. "I didn't know you were going to kill her. Now we're one Sherrerr prisoner down, and a useful one at that. You should have told me what you were going to do."

When Castiel opened his mouth to reply, she held up a hand to silence him. "But I have to admit, you have some interesting skills. Maybe we can find a use for you."

Castiel cursed inwardly. *Enthrall.* He should have tried the Enthrall Cast. What a stupid mistake. He might have been able to force them to answer questions without hurting them. Only he'd been trying too hard to impress Sable.

"There's plenty more I can do," Castiel said. "That's only a small part of it. Let me try again."

"No. I want to think about it before I let you loose on my prisoners again. That's enough for now." Sable yawned. "I'm going back to bed. Come with me."

They left the prisoner cells and returned to the older part of the castle. Sable took Castiel up another flight of stairs. At the top, the servant who had met him at the entrance was waiting.

"Find him a room," Sable told the servant. Then, without saying another word to Castiel, she walked away down the corridor.

In this part of the mountain castle, carpet ran along the floor, softening footsteps and reducing the chill. Castiel followed the servant, but he glanced repeatedly over his shoulder to see what Sable was doing.

She stopped at a room at the far end of the corridor. Four men stood outside it. At first, Castiel thought they were guards, but during one long glance backward, Castiel saw Sable look each man up and down before poking one in the chest. Her choice followed her into her room.

That night, Castiel's thoughts were diverted from his killing of Tremoille to what he'd seen in the corridor. He wondered if one day he would be joining Sable in her room.

CHAPTER ELEVEN

According to the data Carina was seeing from the shuttle's scanners, Dirksen and Sherrerr ships had clearly slogged it out hard for control of Ostillon. As well as the traces of heavy and prolonged pulse fire, it looked like something big had exploded. The interplanetary space was a mess.

She set a trajectory that would take them in the opposite direction from the fast-moving cloud of flotsam.

Cloak was a useful Cast. The shuttle's scanners could receive data yet other ships' scanners were apparently not picking up their presence. Otherwise the ships in the vicinity would be giving them five seconds to explain themselves.

How long would the Cloak last? Carina was about to leave the controls to go and ask Darius when she heard someone run up behind her. Before she could turn to see who it was, she was slapped across the back of her head. Carina spun around and caught Parthenia's arm as she was about to land another blow.

Carina stood up, maintaining her grip on her sister's arm. They locked gazes. Carina released Parthenia. Her sister hit her again, slapping her forcefully across the face. Carina bore the attack as Parthenia continued to rain blows on her head and face. She didn't defend herself.

Parthenia's fist split Carina's gum across her tooth and hot blood oozed into her mouth. Her ear rang from Parthenia hitting it. Then her sister landed a blow on the bridge of her nose. Blood burst out and ran down her face. The pain brought tears to her eyes.

Eventually Bryce realized what was happening and ran into the cabin. He grabbed Parthenia's shoulders and pulled her away from Carina. She didn't resist.

"What the hell do you think you're doing?" Bryce said.

Parthenia didn't take her eyes off Carina. She took a step closer. Bryce inserted his arm between them to prevent her from resuming her attack.

"Don't ever speak to me again," Parthenia hissed at Carina. She turned and stalked out of the cabin.

"Stars, you're a mess," said Bryce. "I'll find something to help you clean up. Are you okay?"

"I'm fine."

Carina sat down and put her head in her hands. Blood dripped from her nose onto the console. "I don't blame her. It's no more than I deserve."

"No more than you deserve? She should be on her knees thanking you for saving her life. She would have died on Ostillon by herself."

"I know, but what I did was wrong. She's old enough to decide for herself what risks she wants to take. I just couldn't bear to lose her. Not after what happened to Ma. I was being selfish. Now she'll hate me forever, justifiably."

"At least she'll be alive," said Bryce. "I can understand she would be angry, but she's overreacting. She has to know you did it for her own good."

Carina pressed her sleeve against her nose to stem the flow of blood. "You don't understand. Casting Enthrall on another mage goes against everything we stand for. It's a Cast you're only really supposed to use in self-defense. It's entirely against our code to use it to gain advantage over someone, especially another mage. Double-especially your own family. I guess Ma made that clear to them at some point. What I did was far worse than abandoning Parthenia to her fate. I wouldn't be surprised if the rest of them hated me now as well."

"I'm sure they don't, and that Parthenia will come around eventually. If they hate you for saving their sister from Castiel, they're a bunch of idiots."

Carina smiled and then regretted it as her cut gum sent out a sliver of pain. Her nose hurt like a bitch too. "They're only kids, Bryce, and they were protected from the harsh realities of life as they were growing up. When you consider that, they've all done amazingly well over the last few weeks. I'm proud of them."

"If you say so. I'll try to find a cloth and some water."

Carina hoped that the shuttle was stocked with

water and other emergency supplies. As it was a military vessel, she would have been surprised if it wasn't, but it was a possibility. The vessel was so old it had probably been brought out of storage for the battle. She hoped it contained what they would need to sustain them during their trip to their next destination, wherever that might be.

She checked the fuel level and was gratified to see it was registering one hundred percent. Next, she checked the shuttle's range. Her heart sank. The little vessel would not take them far. She brought up the local region's star map and drew a sphere at the boundary of the farthest the shuttle would take them without refueling.

"Bryce asked me to help you," said Nahla, standing at the cabin doorway. She was holding a piece of cloth and a water ration.

Carina had hardly spoken to the little girl since rescuing her from Langley Dirksen's mansion. Little Nahla had been constantly quiet and submissive, meekly going along with whatever they did. Carina hadn't even asked her if she was pleased she had taken her away from Castiel.

"Thanks," Carina said.

Nahla moved closer and dampened the cloth with water from the container before carefully dabbing at the drying blood on Carina's face. She touched Carina's nose, which made Carina suck in a breath and wince. Nahla drew away in fear.

"It's okay," said Carina. "It just hurts a bit." As Nahla resumed her gentle cleaning, Carina asked, "What's Bryce doing?"

"He's talking to Parthenia."

It was nice of him but Carina doubted it would

do any good. She knew that in Parthenia's position she would have reacted just the same, if not worse.

"Are you glad you aren't with Castiel anymore?" Carina asked, hoping that at least one of her half-siblings didn't despise her.

"Yes, I am. I thought he was a nice brother, but he was mean to me. I didn't want to stay with him anymore."

"That's good to hear, Nahla. Thank you."

The little girl blushed and looked down, unused to receiving approval.

Stefan Sherrerr had screwed up his offspring in so many different ways.

***

"Not another freezing trip," Oriana whined.

Their shuttle had departed the Floria system, and Carina was explaining their destination options. Only two star systems with inhabited planets were within range and to reach either of them would entail a reenactment of their flight from the *Nightfall*, where they had endured life support set at the minimum level for survival to eke out the fuel.

"We don't have a lot of choice about it," Carina snapped. Her nose continued to throb. She wondered if it was broken.

Parthenia hated her, and now she realized she'd persuaded her family to leave Ostillon only to face the prospect of a dangerous journey and an uncertain arrival. "So, which is it to be? The ship's data banks don't carry much information on either system. Both have only one habitable planet, and they're both backwater places, which is good."

"Huh," said Bryce. "You mean like Ostillon?"

"Right," Carina sighed. "Like I thought Ostillon was. So I guess we have no idea what the hell we're going to find."

"I vote we go to whichever is closest in that case," Ferne said.

"There's only three or four days' difference in traveling time," Carina said. "The one that's farthest away seems a slightly better bet to me. Its name is Pirine. The nearer one is mostly rock. That's called Goania. The inhabitants might have to ration water."

"But do these worlds belong to the Sherrerrs or the Dirksens?" asked Parthenia. "Isn't that the most important question we should be asking?"

"The ship's database is way outdated," Carina replied. "But according to that, both systems are neutral, which really means they're disputed, as we know. But what difference does it make? Both clans are after us. Maybe I should try to take you out of this galactic sector entirely. Now the Sherrerrs and the Dirksens know about mages, it may be the only way you'll ever be safe."

"I'm not doing that," Parthenia said. "As soon as I can, I'm returning to Ostillon to find Castiel. And if he's left the planet I'm going to search for him. I'm not going to rest until I make sure he'll never hurt anyone again."

"I haven't given up on doing that either," Carina said. "Just not with you guys in tow."

Parthenia refused to acknowledge Carina's words.

"I vote we go to the closest planet," Oriana said. "The rocky one. The less time we spend freezing in space the better."

"But we need water for Casting," said Carina. "If it's in short supply, that could make things difficult for us."

"Then as soon as we've refueled," Oriana said, "we leave for Pirine."

"Pirine isn't anywhere near Goania," said Carina. "That's why I wanted to talk to you about it now. We're hanging in space outside the Floria system. Once we make a decision we can't change our minds. Do you know how much it costs to fuel even a little, ancient ship like this? After we arrive at the new place, assuming we aren't detected and manage to hide the shuttle, it will take us months to work and save enough money for another journey. Whatever we decide now has to be the right choice."

Carina was beginning to rethink her decision to open the question of their destination to her brothers and sisters. She'd wanted to include them in the planning more because she was feeling bad over what she'd done to Parthenia.

She was also wondering if she'd done the right thing in escaping Ostillon. News of their escape must have gotten back to Castiel, and ships would be searching for the fine trace of a single, small shuttle fleeing the system.

Bryce had been silent for the discussion but he finally spoke. "In my opinion, you're over thinking it. We don't know enough to make an informed decision and we have no way of finding out any more information. Pirine could be a secret Sherrerr military base and Goania could be a Dirksen prison planet for all we know. Just pick one and we'll go there. We'll have to take whatever comes to us no matter what."

"So, Goania?" Carina asked.

"I guess so," Bryce replied.

"Yes, Goania," Oriana said.

Ferne nodded.

Darius said, "I want to go wherever you think is best, Carina."

"I don't mind," said Nahla.

"I vote we return to Ostillon," said Parthenia.

"I'm sorry, but that isn't an option," Carina said. "Looks like Goania it is. I'll set the coordinates. Can you all please scour the ship for whatever you can find to help us get through the next four weeks?"

"Four weeks?!" Oriana was aghast. "That's twice as long as it took us to get to Ostillon."

"We could always go to Pirine," Carina said. "That would take us four and a half weeks."

"Ugh, I hope we find something different from ration bars to eat," replied Oriana.

Carina doubted the shuttle had been stocked with anything else. She only hoped the rations weren't as old as the vessel itself. Leaving the others to figure out how they were going to survive the journey, she returned to the pilot's controls to input Goiania's coordinates and pare down every energy consuming system on the ship to its minimum sustainable level.

They were in for a tough journey, but perhaps arriving at Goania would prove the beginning of a brighter future.

***

The bare interior of the military shuttle didn't make for the best sleeping quarters, but the vessel contained emergency gear and the children had sufficient imagination to make tolerable beds from it in the narrow aisles between seats. Carina set the quiet and active shifts. It helped to have a routine and well-defined 'days' and 'nights' to keep them from descending into apathy and depression. In the quiet shift, Carina and Bryce slept next to each other for warmth and the girls and boys similarly huddled up.

There wasn't much to do except sleep. They didn't have the ingredients to make elixir and the supply that they had was precious. They needed to save it so that Darius could Cloak the ship again when they landed on Goania. After that, they might need all the Casts they could muster to remain safe.

Carina grew to enjoy settling into Bryce's arms to sleep. The physical closeness of him was her only comfort. She was wracked with self-doubt over what she was doing and fear for the lives of her siblings. Parthenia still wasn't talking to her, though the rest of her siblings didn't appear to also hate her guts. Nonetheless if that was what it took to keep them alive she would bear it.

One quiet shift, soon after she dozed off, *Carina found herself on the grassy plain once more. She immediately recognized the place. She knew she'd been here many times before. She also knew she was dreaming. How come she didn't recall these dreams when she awoke?*

The plain was empty and all she could hear was the wind in the grass. Feeling eyes on her back, Carina spun around. There they were. In the distance, the familiar figures were toiling in her direction. Again, she saw the extremely old woman swathed in robes, the almost-giant of a man with a long beard, and the childlike figure.

They seemed far away, however. The last time she'd seen them they had been closer, so close that the old woman had been able to look her in the eyes.

Where was she? And why did she keep returning to this place regularly when she slept? Carina set off walking through the grass toward the people in the distance. Perhaps if she could meet them she could ask them for an explanation. She walked quickly, wading through the thigh-high grass. She didn't know how long she would remain asleep. Time seemed to pass differently in the dream world.

But though Carina strode as fast as she could, she didn't draw any nearer to the group. If anything, she appeared to be moving away from them. Forcing her way through the high grass was hard. She halted while she caught her breath. Her gaze remained on the walking people, and as she watched she frowned. Though she was still and they were walking toward her, they were actually growing more distant.

What was happening? The uniform, grassy plain seemed to be growing wider as she watched. She would have to run if she wanted to draw close to them, run faster than the expansion of the plain.

"We're going the wrong way!"

Someone was shouting in Carina's ear. Someone she knew.

Darius. What was he doing on the plain?

Carina woke up. Her covering had fallen off and

the chill cabin air was invading her bones. Darius was hovering next to her, the same as he had been in her dream, though he was shadowy in the dim cabin, not brightly lit by a hot sun as he'd been a moment previously.

"We're going the wrong way," Darius repeated. "I didn't understand."

Bryce began to wake.

Carina sat up. "Not so loud. Everyone's trying to sleep."

"We have to turn around," said Darius.

"We can't turn around. We...Come with me." She took a cover and wrapped it around herself before going into the pilot's cabin, bringing Darius along.

"Did you have a bad dream?" she asked after closing the door.

"No, I didn't. I had a nice dream. I'm sorry, Carina. It's all my fault. I didn't understand, and I kept forgetting. And then when we were talking about where to go next, I didn't want to say anything because I wanted to do whatever you decided. But now they're telling me I made a mistake."

"They're telling you? Who are telling you?"

"The people in the *dream*," Darius explained, as if Carina was a little simple-minded.

"What people? Wait." Carina noticed Darius was shaking with cold. "Come here." She wrapped her arms around him so that the blanket covered them both. "What have you been dreaming about?"

Though Darius didn't seem to have had a nightmare, he'd clearly dreamt something that had gotten him worked up and confused.

"I can't remember very well, but I'm in a new place. Outside in a field. There are people there talking to me. One of them's an old lady. She talks to me a lot, but I can't remember most of what she says. Only that we need to go to the planet with the numbers. I remembered that when we were deciding where to go, but I didn't want to say anything. I thought it was just a dream. Then tonight she was cross with me. She said we're going the wrong way and we have to turn around."

"Okay, I get it," said Carina. Darius was worried and stressed and it was affecting his sleep. It wasn't surprising, given everything that had happened. His anxiety was playing out in his dreams. She hugged her brother tightly. "I hear what you're saying, sweetheart, but it's too late for us to turn around now. We have to go to Goania because we don't have enough fuel to get us anywhere else. But it's going to be okay, Darius."

"No!" Her brother struggled free from her arms and faced her. "We have to go to the planet with the numbers."

"What do you mean? That doesn't make any sense."

"The woman said we must go to the planet that has the numbers."

Numbers? Darius had been drawing numbers almost obsessively for weeks. Carina decided to humor him. "What numbers? Do you want to show me?" She opened the pilot's interface and brought up the keyboard. "Type them here."

Darius tapped three sets of numbers onto the screen. Carina's chest tightened. She hadn't taken much notice of her brother's scrawlings, but seeing the numbers on an interface made her realize immediately that they looked like galactic coordinates. What was more, the coordinates looked familiar. Her heart sinking, Carina looked up Pirine's coordinates. They were the same.

Noticing her expression, or perhaps absorbing her feeling, Darius' chin trembled. "I was right, wasn't I? The planet with the numbers is the one we were supposed to be going to. And I didn't tell you."

"It's okay. It's okay." Carina hugged her brother again while she thought things over. "Darius, who told you where we were supposed to go?" A tingling of familiarity was teasing her mind. She'd been dreaming too when Darius had woken her up. For a moment she'd thought he was part of her dream.

"The old lady," Darius replied. "But there were other people there too. I'm not sure how many."

"The old lady?" The thought of an older woman also rang a bell in Carina's mind.

The cabin door opened. Bryce was standing there, a blanket over his shoulders and his hair ruffed up. "Is everything all right?"

"Yeah, we're okay," said Carina. "You can go back to sleep."

"But we have to turn around," Darius almost yelled. His little body stiffened in Carina's arms.

"I told you," she said, "we can't. Maybe after we arrive at Goania we can refuel after a few weeks and then go to Pirine."

"Why would we want to go to Pirine?" asked Bryce. He stepped into the cabin and closed the door.

"Someone in Darius' dreams is telling him to go there. He even knew the coordinates." Carina nodded at the interface screen.

Bryce peered at the numbers. "Holy shit. That's weird."

"You're telling me. And the weirdest thing is, I think I might have been having a similar dream."

"Well, that's...." Bryce paused. He touched the cabin wall. "Hey, have we stopped?"

"Huh?" Carina said. Then she noticed it too. The slight vibration of a spaceship in motion was absent. The shuttle's engine had stopped. She wiped Pirine's coordinates from the interface and brought up the operations display.

The engine was offline. But why? They had enough fuel for another two weeks' travel. Had something gone wrong somewhere? Carina ran a diagnostic. Everything was fine, except.... She groaned. The fuel level read one hundred percent. It was impossible considering the distance they'd traveled. The gauge was faulty. They shuttle must have been carrying far less fuel than she'd thought when they set out. They hadn't had enough fuel to get them anywhere.

"What's wrong?" asked Bryce.

The Dirksens had only been using the shuttle to transport troops to and from the planet surface. They hadn't required the vessel to travel long distances. As long as the fuel was topped up, it didn't matter that they didn't know exactly how much the vessel was carrying. The mechanics were probably waiting until after the battle was over before fixing the fault.

"Carina," Bryce said, "why have we stopped?"

"We're out of fuel."

"What? How come?"

Shit. Shit. Shit. "This ship's a piece of junk, that's how come."

She brought up their position. The display said exactly what she knew it would say. They were halfway to Goania, in deep space, and far from any trade routes.

There was a click and the display flashed, *Main fuel supply exhausted. Emergency backup supply activated. Minimal life support only.* They were already running on minimal life support.

Carina did the only thing possible in the situation. It was better to be picked up than to die in the loneliness of space, even if their rescuer was a Sherrerr or a Dirksen. The chances anyone would come within range to notice the signal were slim, but it was their only hope.

She turned on the distress beacon.

CHAPTER TWELVE

Castiel woke to a chilly atmosphere in his room in the Dirksens' mountain castle. He had fallen asleep quickly after leaving Sable Dirksen, tired after the previous day's events. He didn't know how long he'd slept. The room had no windows and contained nothing to tell him the time.

He turned on the light. The room's walls were rough hewn from the pale gray mountain stone. A smaller version of the fireplace Castiel had seen in the great hall occupied the central spot on the wall opposite the bed, its grate bare. In a corner stood a wash-basin, also roughly cut from the mountain's stone. A spigot overhung the basin. In another corner sat a clothes chest. A mirror hung on the wall. And that was it. Castiel concluded that Sable Dirksen rarely hosted guests, and that when she did she took little care to spoil them with luxury.

He rose from his bed, dressed himself, and took his bottle of elixir out from underneath the covers where it had lain all night. The bottle was warmed by his body heat and he found it reassuring to hold. He would have to arrange the making of a plentiful supply soon. He had taught one of Langley's servants the method and he would do the same in his new habitation.

Castiel suddenly halted on his way to the door. Should he tell Sable about his need for elixir? It seemed unavoidable. Anyone with half a brain would notice that he always took a sip of the liquid before he Cast. How much more about being a mage should he tell her, however? Whatever he told her could give her control over him, and that was the last thing he wanted. He wasn't prepared to become another clan lackey, a tool to do their bidding. If the Dirksens wanted to make use of his services, they would have to show him the respect he deserved.

Castiel shivered. The castle really was cold, as Sable had complained. He was surprised that the Dirksens, with their love of high-tech, had failed at adequately heating the place.

He opened the door and nearly walked into the guard who was standing directly outside. For a few moments Castiel feared the man would try to prevent him from leaving, but the guard only offered to take him to Sable.

She was sitting where he'd first seen her, next to a fire in the great hall of the castle. She was alone again, but this time she was dressed. Sable Dirksen's dark tunic flared out at the shoulders and overhung narrow pants. She looked far more like the head of the Dirksen clan that morning than she had the previous night, though she still seemed ridiculously young for the position. Castiel judged it unwise to voice his impressions.

Another armchair had been added opposite Sable's as well as a small table on which breakfast dishes stood. Castiel sat down at the armchair without being invited, determined to maintain an attitude of confidence and control.

"Good morning," he said as he helped himself to breakfast.

Sable's dark-eyed gaze flicked at him. "How did you sleep?"

"Well, thank you." He was amusedly reminded of the conversational style of his father and mother. So much had passed unsaid between them. "Though my room was cold."

"Ah, yes. We've never been able to heat this older section of the castle adequately. The stone seems to suck all warmth out of the air no matter what heating devices we install. I keep a fire lit here all the time."

Castiel continued to eat while he considered how best to approach the subject of his desired role in the Dirksen clan.

"I'm curious to learn more about the ability you demonstrated last night," said Sable. "How did you kill that Sherrerr admiral?"

"It's just something I can do. Among many other things."

"Like what?"

Castiel put down his plate. "I'd rather talk about your plans for me."

"It's hard to make any plans unless I know how I can use you."

"If you tell me more about what the Dirksens

intend to accomplish, I could explain how I can help."

"We intend many things. Apart from killing people in a rather horrible way, what else do you have to offer?"

Castiel pursed his lips and stared at Sable. They were already at stalemate and they'd barely been talking for one minute.

But then the Dirksen clan leader raised a finger to her ear and leaned slightly forward as if listening. "Send him in," she said, adding, to Castiel, "You can stay."

This permission-giving irked Castiel. He felt his status was above being told when he could remain or leave, but he resigned himself to bearing the insult for the time being.

A shaven-headed officer in a Dirksen uniform entered the hall. He took in Castiel's presence with a brief glance as he strode to stand in front of Sable and saluted. "I am honored to formally convey the news that our forces have successfully repulsed the Sherrerr attack, ma'am. Shortly after the *Nightfall* self-destructed, the rest of the Sherrerr fleet departed. A thorough check of the system has discovered no enemy ships."

"Thank you, Commander Kee. That is good news." Sable paused, then added. "Commander, I would like to introduce you to Castiel Sherrerr."

The man quickly suppressed his look of surprise and delivered a curt nod to Castiel.

"He's been on Ostillon for some time, staying at Langley Dirksen's residence. I believe I'm correct in saying that he has renounced his affiliation with his clan?" Sable looked toward Castiel for confirmation.

"Yes, of course," Castiel blurted.

"Perhaps you're wondering if he's connected to the young merc in the Sherrerr shuttle you picked up?" Sable asked the commander. "The answer is yes. From what I understand, the two are related. He gave me a demonstration of his strange power last night when I asked him to interrogate a prisoner. He killed her."

"*Killed*, ma'am?" Kee's eyebrows lifted.

"The commander is one of our top interrogators," Sable explained to Castiel. "It seems he also disapproves of your methods."

"That was...hasty of me, I admit," Castiel said. "But I have other things I can try, if you'll give me a second chance."

"Uh..." said Commander Kee, clearly dying to object but unable to break protocol and speak without first being addressed. "Permission to—"

"Don't worry, Commander. I won't be letting him loose on any more of our precious prisoners just yet. Not until I have a much better understanding of what he does. While you're here, why don't you go and see what you can find out from the remaining ones? When they hear their friends have departed and they're alone without a hope of rescue they might feel more inclined to divulge something."

"Yes, ma'am."

Kee saluted and left them, striding toward the exit that led to the lower level.

"Castiel," said Sable, "I feel like we've gotten off on the wrong foot. Why don't we try again? Would you like me to show you around my abode? It's quite an unusual residence, isn't it?"

"I-I'd like that," replied Castiel, somewhat taken aback by her sudden change of attitude.

"Come with me. We'll start at the peak." Sable rose and led Castiel across the hall to a small elevator. "I had to have this put in when I arrived," she said as the doors opened. "The castle floors rise to the very top of the mountain, but all there was to move between them was stairs. Can you believe it?"

They stepped inside the elevator and the doors closed.

"So what I was thinking was correct," said Castiel. "The Dirksens didn't build this place."

"That's right. We squeezed the secret of its existence inadvertently from an Ostillonian official. I forget who it was. He thought the information might buy him some clemency. He was wrong. I found the castle perfect for my needs, however, so I moved in. I've added some sections since then."

Castiel surveyed Sable from the corners of his eyes. He knew the Dirksens had taken over the planet several years previously. How old had their leader been then? She had to be older than she looked.

They rode the elevator to the top floor, and the doors opened to reveal a small, round room encircled by narrow, arched windows without glass. They stepped out and Castiel immediately walked to a window. A keen wind blew through it. The view was magnificent. They were at the very top of the mountain and he could see for miles all around.

"It's certainly something, right?" Sable said. "I

come up here sometimes to think."

"But doesn't this place give away the fact that there's something inside the mountain? Aren't you worried someone looking at the mountain range could spot it?"

"It isn't visible from the outside, the same as the entrance you flew in through."

"That's amazing. I don't think the Sherrerrs have that tech yet."

Sable gave a small chuckle. "We don't have that tech either. It's how the place was when we arrived. We needed precise directions from the Ostillonian to find it. He said the few locals who know about it don't talk of it because they think the place is cursed. I have to say, considering the problems we have with heating it, sometimes I'm inclined to agree."

They spent a few minutes gazing at the view before descending to the level below. As the morning progressed, Castiel saw most of the castle. Several of the rooms rose stories high. These were the coldest parts of the castle and they were entirely bare, as if Sable never used them. She also showed him many rooms and suites for sleeping and living, and the usual service areas. While they were walking the corridors they passed servants and people in rich clothes. Though Sable nodded greetings at the latter, she did not introduce Castiel to them. He guessed they were high-ranking Dirksens.

He was impressed by the size and intricacy of the place, as well as mildly curious about who had constructed it. One thing he noticed was that all of the residential areas contained spigots, even though the restrooms were plentiful. In all, however, he found himself becoming bored. He imagined there were more exciting and influential things he could be doing if Sable would allow him.

As they walked, Sable asked Castiel about his experiences at Langley Dirksen's estate. He guessed that she was mining him for information on Langley's behavior regarding him. Though she didn't give much away, Castiel understood that Langley had misled Sable about how long he'd stayed at her mansion and what he'd done. He didn't hesitate to set Sable right. He felt no loyalty to Langley whatsoever. She had stymied his attempts to rise in the Dirksen hierarchy.

When they returned to the great hall, Commander Kee was awaiting them.

"Commander," said Sable, "did you find out anything useful?"

"Not yet, ma'am," he replied. "I hope you don't mind, but I took the liberty of removing the remains of the dead prisoner. I'm afraid to say the death has probably set back my work for several weeks." His face was rigid as he steadfastly refused to look at Castiel.

"I'm sorry to hear it," said Sable, "but it can't be helped. Please continue to work with the officers this afternoon. In the meantime, would you join us for lunch?"

"I would be delighted, ma'am."

"Castiel, please take a seat while I make the arrangements. Kee, come with me." Sable left with the commander.

Castiel sat down, wondering if the Dirksen leader had taken Kee into her room at night. As he watched her leave, he again hoped to be one of the chosen. He was young, but he was already growing a beard. Perhaps in time Sable would come to respect and desire him.

***

Castiel spent the next half hour watching servants prepare for a formal lunch. They brought in straight-backed chairs and a table, and spread the table with a cloth before setting out the dining wear. Castiel wasn't impressed by the finery, if that was Sable's intention. His upbringing had made him used to such things. He grew bored. He was tempted to Transport something out of a servant's hands just to make them jump. But he decided against the idea. He didn't want to waste elixir until he had a stable supply.

Finally, when the servants had brought in the food and drinks, Sable and Commander Kee returned. Sable invited Castiel to join them.

A servant filled Castiel's glass with wine, to his great pleasure. The Dirksen leader was treating him like an adult. He lifted the glass and took a large gulp of the alcohol. It didn't taste as good as he'd thought it would, but he enjoyed the pleasant, hot feeling as the liquid slid down his throat into his stomach.

When the servants had uncovered all the dishes, they withdrew.

Castiel took another large swallow of wine. An unfamiliar wooziness began to invade his mind. Over the brim of his glass, he noticed Kee watching him. Was he drinking too much? Castiel set down his glass.

"Please help yourself," she said to Castiel. "I

hope you don't mind no servants waiting on us. I hate having people hovering around me as I eat."

"I don't mind," Castiel said. "Though I'm used to servants."

"I guess you must be," said Kee, "as one of the most important members of the Sherrerrs."

"Oh, I wasn't...." Castiel paused, uncertain as to what would be most beneficial for him to tell them regarding his position in the Sherrerr hierarchy. From things his father had said, he'd guessed that his family hadn't been as important as Father would have liked. But that had changed on the *Nightfall*, when Carina and the others had blown up the Dirksen shipyard. "I mean, yes, that's right."

"Your clan must be feeling your loss acutely, I imagine," Sable said.

"Yes, they must be," said Castiel. "Acutely. They don't have any mages on their side anymore, you see."

Was that a flicker of a glance between Sable and Kee? Castiel wasn't sure, but it didn't matter. They might think they'd won a tidbit of information, but he was feeling suddenly generous.

He took a spoonful of food from a dish and piled it on his plate. The wine and the cold of the castle were making him hungry. Sable and Kee also ate and drank a little wine.

"We guessed the Sherrerrs had some kind of special advantage over us," Sable said. "We've known it for years. The problem was figuring out what it was. I'm glad you're here to enlighten us."

"I'm not only here to enlighten you, I'm here to help you. The *Nightfall* is only one example of what

I can do. There's plenty more I have to offer…for the right price," Castiel said, his confidence swelling. Now they were finally having the conversation that he'd wanted all along.

"Why don't you begin by telling us all about mages?" said Kee. "I don't know anything about them."

"Mages?" Castiel said. "Where do I start? Let me think for a moment." He drank some more wine. He felt dizzy and relaxed. "Well, it's an ability that runs in families. My mother was a mage—"

"Was?" Kee interjected.

"Yes. Both of my parents are dead. Anyway, I inherited my ability from her."

"Fascinating," said Kee, resting his chin on steepled fingertips. "Tell me more."

Castiel, gratified to have Sable and Kee's full attention, told them everything he remembered from eavesdropping on his mother's lessons. He told them about all the Casts he knew, and elixir, and the Characters, and even the snippets about Seasons and other stuff that he'd gleaned, though those parts hadn't made much sense to him.

Sable and Kee listened quietly as he spoke, only interrupting to ask for clarification or more details. Castiel's sense of self-importance grew and he began to embellish his descriptions with stories of services that he'd performed for the Sherrerrs. In truth, it had been Parthenia who had performed most of the feats he described, but if his abilities had developed earlier *he* would have done them so that didn't matter.

Feeling hungry, Castiel wound down and began

to eat his food, which had grown cold on his plate.

"Thank you," said Kee. "That was very enlightening. Just one more thing. You have sisters and brothers who are mages too, if I'm not mistaken?"

Castiel's mouth was full so he only nodded. He'd deliberately left out any mention of Carina and the others. He hadn't wanted Sable or Kee to get the idea that any of his siblings were more valuable to them than himself.

"Langley told me that you have at least three sisters," said Sable. "and we're aware of a much younger boy who I presume is your brother."

Castiel swallowed. "I have another brother too. But you don't need them. They can't do as much as I can."

"I believe I've met one of your sisters myself," said Kee. "But even if your siblings' abilities aren't as great as yours they're a danger to us nevertheless. Do you know what's happened to them? Are they still on Ostillon?"

"I've been searching for signs of them, but I haven't turned up anything yet."

"What sort of signs?" asked Kee.

"It would be reports of extraordinary events, like fires starting for no reason, or people appearing out of thin air. But the war eclipsed all the news reports. I haven't noticed anything I thought worth pursuing. Though I doubt they've left the planet. No domestic ships have departed Ostillon since the Sherrerr attack began, right? I was waiting for the war to end so I could comb the planet for them. They can't hide forever."

Kee frowned. "I heard a strange report only

yesterday, not long after the *Nightfall* was destroyed. A company sergeant said the shuttle transport his soldiers were to board disappeared while it was on the ground at the spaceport. They were going to be court martialed, but when the officials checked the camera footage, the vessel did seem to disappear. Could your siblings have had something to do with that?"

"An entire shuttle?" Castiel thought about it. He guessed it was possible that Carina might have been able to Transport an entire space vessel. But then the soldiers would have seen the shuttle move, not disappear. Then he remembered their flight from the *Nightfall*, after Mother had killed Father. Darius had babbled something about how he'd 'done it.' *Damn*. Had Darius made his special Cast again? "It might be possible."

Kee cursed. "I bet they've returned to the Sherrerrs."

"No," Castiel said. "They would never do that. If they have left Ostillon, they've only run away. We won't be seeing them again." He was annoyed. He'd hoped to use his siblings for his own ends, but in some ways he was better off without them. Now the Dirksens only had one mage at their disposal, he had more control.

"I wouldn't be too sure of that," said Sable. "If these people aren't here and working with us, they're a liability. I'm not going to be happy as long as I know these mages are roaming the galaxy. Kee, I want you to find them. Find out which vessel went missing. Scan the outer system and the heliopause. None of the Sherrerr ships will leave a trace like a shuttle's. Hopefully, whatever

Castiel's brother did it won't last forever and you'll be able to detect something. Follow the trace. They'll be at the end of it."

"If you send a ship after them I should be on it," said Castiel. "They're mages. You'll need my help to capture them."

"You think they could defeat a destroyer with these Casts you told us about?" Kee asked.

"No, but…" It was unlikely that even Carina could repel a large military craft, and Castiel was reluctant to give the impression that any one of his siblings' powers were stronger than his own.

"I think we can manage," said Sable with a condescending smile. "Please get on it now, Kee."

"Yes, ma'am." The commander stood and left the hall.

If the Dirksens did find Castiel's siblings, he knew he would have to be very careful. He would have to ensure his brothers and sisters remained under *his* control and not the Dirksens'. He also had to watch out that they didn't try to usurp his new position in the clan.

Castiel was about to take another sip of wine, but his stomach felt bad. His wooziness had increased, and a horrible feeling was creeping over him. He put down his fork. He didn't feel at all well, and he couldn't remember exactly what he'd told Sable and Kee. The details were hazy, but he suspected he might have told them more than was wise.

All of a sudden, saliva flooded into Castiel's mouth. He only just had time to turn his head and lean over before he vomited. A sour mix of wine and half-digested food poured out of him in great gushes, splattering on the stone floor and splashing onto his legs.

Hot shame and tears welled up, but there was nothing Castiel could do to stop the humiliating event. His experiences at Sable Dirksen's headquarters were definitely not turning out so well after all.

CHAPTER THIRTEEN

The news that the shuttle was out of fuel and they were adrift went down about as well as Carina expected.

Oriana wailed, "Noooo!"

Parthenia gave Carina a sour look that said, *So you thought you were saving me?*

Ferne was silent and stoic. Nahla didn't seem to know how was best to react.

Darius said, "I'm sorry I didn't tell you, Carina."

"You don't have anything to be sorry for," she replied.

"Sorry you didn't tell her what?" Oriana asked. "Does that mean we could have avoided this?"

"It's nothing," said Carina. "Just a dream Darius was having. He thinks we should have gone to Pirine."

"Well, should we?" asked Oriana. "What kind of dream?"

"Look, we're here now," Carina said. "There's no point in talking about what ifs. Our distress signal will be picked up eventually and someone will come along and save us. We have plenty of rations and water. We only have to be patient and wait."

Carina was trying to be more upbeat than she felt. She'd deliberately left out the fact that they were in the middle of nowhere, in sparsely trafficked space where cargo transporters and other inter-system craft rarely traveled. Telling her family more than they needed to know served no purpose and would only make them more afraid.

"So we can look forward to even more weeks of this?" asked Oriana. "I'm not sure I can stand it."

"You're going to have to stand it," Carina snapped.

"Yes," said Ferne. "Stop whining, Oriana. I'm sick of your constant complaints."

Oriana's face fell at this rare rebuke from her twin. She stood up and stalked away. As there were very few places for her to stalk to, realistically, she faced the bulkhead with her arms folded.

Ferne rolled his eyes but didn't otherwise react. In the end it was little Nahla who went to attend to Oriana's sulk. She put a hand on her sister's back and also faced the wall, perhaps to offer some companionship. Oriana didn't react but tolerated the little girl's presence.

"Okay," Carina said. "Let's make a start by figuring out how few ration bars we can eat a day and still survive. We haven't been keeping count because we thought we had plenty to last us. But we should think about how many we need to not feel too hungry."

"We should make a cleaning schedule too," said Bryce. "We haven't been cleaning up after ourselves and it shows. This place is disgusting."

"You're right," Carina said. "Great idea." Bryce's suggestion made her feel a bit less alone in her responsibility to save all their lives.

"Aww, I hate cleaning," said Darius.

"How would you know?" Parthenia asked. "You've never cleaned anything in your life. None of us have, really. We always had servants to do that kind of thing."

Carina tensed. Was Parthenia going to start complaining now too?

But her sister continued, "So now's a good time to start. I'll put together a rota."

Carina thanked her, but Parthenia pretended she hadn't heard.

The meeting broke up. Carina was wondering if she should talk to Oriana when an alarm sounded in the pilot's cabin. She groaned. What had gone wrong now? Giving Bryce a worried look, she went to find out.

The scanners indicated a ship was approaching them. For a moment, Carina couldn't believe it. How was it possible that another vessel had heard their distress signal so quickly? She was about to shout out the joyful news when a realization hit her. The ship had not hailed them, and it was almost impossible that their signal had been picked up so quickly.

What was far more likely was that the ship had been on their tail, and now the shuttle had stopped the pursuers had caught up.

Just when she was thinking they were in a bad

way, things had gotten even worse.

"What is it?" Bryce asked as he entered the cabin.

"Enemy ship," said Carina. "I'm guessing it's the Dirksens'."

"Are you sure? Maybe it's come to rescue us."

"Not likely. Not so soon. And I can't think of a better explanation for a ship suddenly appearing the minute we stop. Can you?"

"No. So, what do we do?"

Carina was already running through the possible courses of action in her mind. They had enough elixir for a few Casts. They would have no choice about being boarded. The little shuttle carried no weaponry. The question was, what could they do after that to avoid being taken back to Ostillon?

Could they take over an entire ship? It would be hard, probably impossible, but they had to try.

Carina checked the scan readings on the approaching ship. The fact that the vessel wasn't hailing them confirmed her conclusion this was no rescue. She only hoped that Castiel hadn't ordered the Dirksens to blow his siblings to pieces.

But the vessel was a destroyer and already within range to fire. If Castiel had wanted them dead they would be atomized by now. No. He wanted the mages alive and under his control.

"I hope Castiel isn't aboard," said Carina, "or we're screwed. If he isn't, we stand a chance. We can use the remaining elixir to Cast the best we can and take command of the ship."

"You want to try to take command of an entire destroyer?" asked Bryce, who was watching the display.

"Do you have any better ideas? We can't get away from it, and the only alternative to taking it over is to trigger its self-destruct. If we did that we would be right back where we started: adrift with scant hope of rescue"

"I guess you're right."

"Okay, take over the ship is what we do. It'll reach us in a couple of minutes. I have to tell the others what's happening and make a plan."

But as she stepped past Bryce to leave the cabin, he said, "Carina, wait. Look."

She swung around to look again at the display, and her eyes popped. Another ship was approaching. *Two* ships? Carina checked and double-checked the readings, wondering if the faulty fuel gauge wasn't the only problem with the shuttle's instruments. But as far as she could tell the information was accurate.

"What's happening?" Ferne asked, poking his head around the cabin door.

"Uh, I have no idea," Carina replied.

Then the first ship fired on the newcomer.

"What the hell?" Bryce exclaimed.

A beat later the pulse hit. The second ship appeared to survive the blast.

"Are they fighting over us?" asked Bryce. "Is the other one a Sherrerr ship?"

It was the only explanation, but the answer only brought more questions. It was conceivable that the Dirksens had tracked them to their current position by following their trace. Darius' Cloak Cast would have dissipated eventually. But how had the Sherrerrs found them? Or had they been following the Dirksens' destroyer?

The Dirksen ship fired again, and again the pulse impacted the Sherrerr vessel at close quarters. Somehow, the ship withstood the second blow, and once more it didn't return fire. Carina watched the battle curiously. She was more worried about what would happen afterward than which side won. The mages' fate was equally dicey whatever the outcome.

Carina couldn't understand why the Sherrerr ship wasn't returning fire. Its captain didn't seem to be trying to engage in a parley.

Then the readings went crazy. A split second later, something hit the shuttle. The force of the impact threw Carina against the bulkhead. Her back collided with a strut, and the next few minutes were confused chaos as the vessel tumbled over and over. Carina was flung around the pilot's cabin, colliding with Bryce. She put her head down and tucked herself into a ball to minimize the damage to her body.

Finally, the tumbling slowed enough for Carina to grab the back of the pilot's seat and steady herself. Bryce was out cold, bobbing next to the ceiling. Blood welled from a cut on his head, forming a thick pool of red that dispersed in globules. The a-grav was out.

"Bryce." Carina pushed against the shuttle console with her feet to reach him. He moaned and his eyes opened. He was coming around. "Bryce, can you hear me? Are you okay?"

His gaze focused on her. "I'm all right, I think. Head hurts."

Letting go of his shirt, Carina propelled herself

into the main cabin of the slowly spinning vessel. The children were scared and crying. There were several bumps and grazes, but no one seemed to have suffered a serious injury. The piles of makeshift bedding had served as buffers between them and the hard shell of the cabin interior.

"What's going on?" Ferne asked. "Is someone attacking us?"

"I don't know," Carina replied. "I don't think so." If either of the battling ships had wanted to destroy the shuttle they could have done so easily and no one would have had time to register what had happened.

"Carina," Bryce called.

She gripped the handlebars that lined the bulkhead and pulled herself into the pilot's cabin. Bryce was hanging over the controls, droplets of blood suspended in a cloud around his head.

"It's gone," he said. "The destroyer that arrived first. It's been blown to bits."

"So that's what happened," said Carina. "The Sherrerr ship finally fired back. The debris hit us."

A warning flashed on the console display and at the same time yet another alarm began to wail. Carina cursed. The shuttle was leaking atmosphere.

"As if we don't have enough problems." Carina swept the interface with her fingers, bringing up the site of the leak. The shuttle should auto repair, but she wanted to check that it was. "Shit." The vessel hadn't been alerting them to a leak, but *leaks*. The impact of the exploded ship's debris had riddled them full of holes. It was a miracle no one had been hit.

Carina hoped that the Sherrerr ship intended to pick them up quickly. They were losing air so fast, if it didn't they were dead.

She devoted the shuttle's remaining power to atmosphere generation to try to match the loss, or they would all be unconscious in minutes. Meanwhile, she briefed the others on what to do if they were boarded. She hadn't given up on her idea of taking over the enemy ship.

A comm arrived. "Unidentified shuttle prepare to be boarded."

It was odd that the other ship also hadn't identified itself. Carina would have expected a Sherrerr vessel to state its affiliation.

"Are you ready, everyone?" Carina asked.

Darius was going to lead their defense, Enthralling whoever came through the hatch. Then they would have an indefinite amount of time to 'persuade' the Enthralled to give up their weapons and take them to their ship's bridge.

It wouldn't be easy, but they really might be able to do it.

Carina floated on one side of the hatch, waiting. Bryce waited on the other side. The children clung to the backs of seats, doing their best to hide. Darius peaked around his seat, looking nervous.

The hatch lock released and the portal opened.

Carina gave Darius a nod. He nodded back and swallowed elixir before shutting his eyes. People emerged through the shuttle entrance.

Now, Darius.

Her brother cried out and jerked backward, as if impacted by an unseen force.

Carina reeled in shock. What was going on?

Who had Repulsed Darius' Cast? Had Castiel returned to the Sherrerrs?

Bryce propelled himself into the side of one of the boarders, sending the man careening into the others. Carina also pushed off the wall and dove into the melee. She tried to wrest a weapon from its owner's grip. Carina was battling the assailants, spinning in the zero-g.

Suddenly, Carina found herself looking down the wrong end of a muzzle. A curse formed on her lips but she didn't have time to utter it before she was knocked out.

CHAPTER FOURTEEN

Castiel stood in the bright Ostillonian sunlight, hot and angry. Standing on the balcony of a building in the Ostillonian capital, he took a swig of elixir. He concentrated on writing the Transport character, then sent out the Cast toward the roof of a collapsed house. The roof lifted, shedding dust and fragments of plaster, drifted out into the street, and fell to the road with a crash.

Bystanders who had been near the spot where the shattered roof had landed hastily scattered, looking up at Castiel in fear.

He didn't care what the people thought of him. They shouldn't have been standing so near the damaged building. He wished he could Cast some kind of pain or misfortune at them.

Sable had set him the task of helping with the clearing of destroyed and unsafe buildings in the city. When she'd made her request, she'd been extremely flattering, telling him how invaluable his services would be and how much recognition and gratitude he would receive. He'd thought she'd meant recognition and gratitude from the high-ranking Dirksens. Now he understood that in fact she'd meant the people of Ostillon.

What did he care what the lowly folk of that planet thought of him? If he cared anything at all about their feelings, he would have preferred to have their fear and respect, not their gratitude.

It hadn't taken him weeks to realize it had all been a trick. Sable had sidelined him just as smoothly as Langley had, if not more so. At least Langley had arranged for him to have a hand in defeating the Sherrerr attack. Sable seemed intent on making him some kind of glorified janitor or handyman.

It was ridiculous, and he was determined to do something about it. If approaching the head of the clan hadn't worked to elevate his status, he would have to take more drastic measures.

Only he hadn't decided exactly what just yet.

Castiel left the balcony and climbed the stairs to the roof, where a hover vehicle awaited him. He had a few more tasks to complete that day. Though he was loath to do them, he thought he might as well and spend the time figuring out his next steps. It never hurt to practice Casting.

He climbed into the vehicle, and the driver lifted them up over the city. It was indeed a devastated place. Parts of the metropolis had been entirely razed by the Sherrerr attack. In other places great craters opened like wounds, surrounded by charred remains of buildings. The amount of work required to restore the once-thriving capital would be enormous. But it was not his problem.

Castiel recalled the conversation he'd had with Sable in the great hall of her mountain castle the previous evening. He'd tried every well-mannered tactic he could think of to persuade the woman to expand her use of his abilities, but she'd managed to rebuff each point he'd made.

We're devoting our efforts to recuperation and planning at the moment, Sable had said. *When the time is right, I'll introduce you to the rest of the council. I'm sure they will suggest other roles you can play. We need to understand better what you can do and figure out how to fit you into our advancement and expansion. Have some patience, Castiel. Your moment to shine will come.*

It had all sounded reassuring, but Sable had been careful to never mention exactly *when* his moment would come. He wasn't dumb. He knew he was being put off, perhaps indefinitely. Did she fear his powers? He guessed so. Most people did.

The hover vehicle alighted in a street. The place looked like it had been a poor, derelict area even before it had suffered the Sherrerr bombardment. Castiel's task was to demolish an apartment block that had received a direct hit. Half of the building was torn away and the other half was leaning at a dangerous angle.

Castiel looked up at the broken rooms, their contents revealed to the world. Clothes hung from the torn floors. Wall decorations fluttered in the breeze. On the second floor, a corpse sat in a bathtub, a look of surprise on its rotting face.

"Ugh, disgusting," Castiel said.

His driver didn't answer.

There was a knock on Castiel's window. A little

girl was standing there, her face and clothes filthy and her hair a tangle of knots.

"Have you come to rescue my grandpa?" the girl asked, though her voice was muffled by the glass.

Castiel looked down at her rags and then up at her face once more before turning his head away pointedly. The little girl rubbed her eyes and wandered to the rear of the vehicle.

"Please move farther down the street," he instructed the driver.

"The exhaust may burn the child," the driver replied.

"And?" asked Castiel.

The driver opened his door and climbed out.

"My grandpa's stuck in there," said the girl, pointing at the precarious apartment block. "Can you get him out, please?"

The driver shooed her away. He returned to his seat and moved the vehicle another ten meters along the street.

"If the man's been in that building all this time, he must be dead by now," Castiel said, half to himself. He wasn't a law enforcement officer or a splicer. If Sable had wanted to have people rescued, she should have sent someone else.

He swigged his elixir, wrote the Break character, and delivered the Cast to the building remains. The structure began to rumble and shake. The little girl stared at it and screamed. Bricks and concrete began to shatter and fall, and just in time the girl sped out of the way.

Castiel watched the slow, sliding collapse of walls, rooms, and apartments into the street. Clouds of dust rose, obscuring the demolished site.

As the dust began to settle, Castiel looked with pleasure on the pile of rubble that now blocked the street. Only hover vehicles would be able to traverse it. The girl was nowhere to be seen.

Perhaps he should have done a better job. He could Transport some of the rubble away and create a gap. But he would not. If Sable wouldn't bend to persuasion, perhaps he could show enough apparent incompetence to be assigned to different duties. Even doing nothing would be better than his current work.

He'd been cooperative, but maybe the time for being cooperative was over. Sable had seen what he was capable of when he killed Tremoille. She should be more careful about how she treated him, especially if she refused to allow him to rise in the clan. Someone who has nothing, has nothing to lose.

That was the answer. No more playing nice. He would return to the mountain castle and lay it on the line for Sable. Either she would give him a position worthy of his abilities or he would use them against her.

"Take me back to the headquarters," Castiel told the driver.

"I thought we had more assignments, sir," the man said.

"Don't talk back," Castiel yelled. "Do as you're told."

Immediately, the vehicle lifted up from the dusty street. When they were high above the capital, the driver turned and flew them in the direction of the mountains.

***

As the vehicle landed inside the mountain castle, Castiel opened the door and stepped out, intent on confronting Sable. She might be the head of the Dirksen clan, but she was still only one woman, and a young one at that. She was an ordinary human being, while *he* was a mage. She would listen to him or she would suffer for it.

He strode into the great hall. The stone chair was empty as always, but so was Sable's usual seat by the fire, where she would conduct her business via interface or in person. And the fire was out, as if she hadn't been there all day.

A servant who had been cleaning the hall when Castiel entered it, hurried toward an exit.

"Hey, you" Castiel shouted. "Where is Madam Dirksen?"

"I don't know, sir. The mistress left this morning, not long after yourself."

Castiel cursed. He didn't know how to contact her. She hadn't shown him enough respect to tell him. Her disregard for him really was unbearable.

While he hesitated, wondering what to do, Castiel's interface chirruped. He'd received a message. He pulled out the device and read it. The message was from Sable. How had she found out where he was so soon?

> *I see you've returned early, Castiel Sherrerr.*
> *I wanted to speak to you this evening, but something urgent has called me away. I've been thinking about your brothers and sisters. There's still no message from the* Torpille*, the ship that went after the shuttle they stole. I can*

only assume the worst, that somehow they destroyed their pursuer.

Your siblings must be captured and punished for their crime. I'm also concerned about what they might do while at liberty. Perhaps they will gather a force of mages and attack us. I want to prevent this possibility.

I have sent another ship to try to discover what happened to the Torpille.

If the ship is lost, I hope to find out where your siblings went.

Perhaps I should have taken your advice and allowed you to go with the ship.

S.D.

Castiel's anger and frustration drained away. This was more like it. Sable Dirksen was finally recognizing his worth in the clan. He would insist on going along on any further expeditions to discover his siblings' whereabouts. He would be there when they were captured.

With Carina and the others under his control, he would create an entire wing of a new Dirksen force. A mage division. Like it or not, his brothers and sisters would help him cut a swathe through the Sherrerr-controlled areas of the galactic sector. They would be unstoppable. Then, when the time was right, he would make his move and assume control of the Dirksen clan.

Castiel had a vision of four women standing outside his bedroom. All of them beautiful. All for his use. One of the women was Sable Dirksen. He saw himself walk up and down the line, surveying each woman from head to toe. Perhaps, if she was lucky, one night he would choose the former leader of the Dirksen clan.

But that was for the future. Sable's message had calmed him somewhat. He was glad he'd heard from her rather than seen her in person. His anger might have made him hasty and he could have said things he later regretted.

He must remember that though he was a mage, he was alone. He had no guards to command, nowhere secure to sleep. His room had a lock, but that didn't mean he was safe. Someone could still break in and steal his elixir while he slept, leaving him powerless.

He must not let ambition and impatience be his downfall. Father had waited years to play a bigger role in Sherrerr affairs. He must exercise the same restraint.

Yet the days' frustrations had left him tired. Castiel decided to go to his room and lie down while he awaited Sable's return. He left the hall and climbed the cold stone stairs to the corridor that led to his room. When he arrived he was surprised to see the door stood a little ajar. Someone was inside. Was someone searching his things?

But when Castiel stepped into his room, he found that the intruder was only the servant who had been assigned to him. The young woman was preparing his fire.

"Oh, I'm sorry, sir. I wasn't expecting you back so early. I'll finish as quickly as I can and leave you alone."

The good news about Sable's change of attitude had left Castiel feeling generous. "Don't worry.

Take your time." He lay down on his bed and put his hands behind his head. From under half-closed eyes, he watched the young woman pile wood into the grate and light it from underneath.

Castiel had become accustomed to the servant over the weeks that she'd performed her duties for him. He could almost say he liked her. She was always extremely respectful. He didn't think she'd even once looked him in the eye, and she rarely addressed him unless he spoke to her directly.

She was also—he hadn't failed to notice—very pretty.

Castiel watched her languidly, imagining her as one of the women he would line up outside his door. What if he chose her over Sable? Ha! That would make the ex-clan leader spit.

"All done, sir," said the servant, straightening up.

Smoke was rising from the wood and circling lazily up the chimney.

"I hope it warms your room nicely," the young woman continued, keeping her gaze firmly downward. "This place is always so chilly."

The sentences were probably the most the servant had spoken to Castiel at one encounter. He was surprised, and intrigued. She seemed to have a purpose to her loquaciousness, but he couldn't figure out what it was.

"It is cold in this castle," Castiel agreed, sitting up.

The servant lifted her head and looked him directly in the eyes. "Is there anything else I can do for you, sir?"

Castiel's throat tightened. Did she mean what

he thought she meant? Were his fantasies about to become reality? He almost said, *Like what*? but quickly realized what a fool he would sound. Instead, he tried to see how far he could take this potential opportunity. "Actually, there is."

The servant approached him on the bed, her gaze locked onto his. There could be no mistaking her intent. When she reached the bed, she bent down to take off her shoes.

Castiel almost couldn't believe it. It was finally happening. He'd imagined a different kind of scenario, where he would take what he wanted whether the girl agreed to let him or not. So this was strange. But good. Good enough. The servant had to find him irresistible.

She sat on the edge of his bed and began to unfasten her blouse.

CHAPTER FIFTEEN

When Carina woke the first thing she noticed was the familiar vibration of a ship's engine. The boarders must have carried her onto their vessel. She was lying on a padded surface rather than the hard floor of a cell, and she didn't seem to be restrained. Good. The Sherrerrs who had captured them were clearly idiots.

Carina opened her eyelids to slits. The room she was in was white and brightly lit. She could hear someone moving around, but she couldn't see the person due to the angle of her head. Her eyes faced the corner of the ceiling. She didn't want to move or her captors would know she was awake. If they thought she remained unconscious they might say something significant.

In the end, it was Darius' voice she heard.

"Ow! Don't do that! No!"

Carina was up in an instant. She launched herself in the direction of her brother's voice. Darius was lying on his front on a bed, and someone was leaning over him and touching his hair. Carina leapt onto the man's back and grabbed his forehead and chin before wrenching his head around, trying to break his neck.

"Whaaaaa! Argh!" The man stumbled backward, sending Carina crashing into the wall. The man stumbled forward. Carina clung onto his back, feeling for his eyes. Together, they fell into some equipment. The metal implements scattered over the floor. The man fell down and rolled onto his back, trying to dislodge her.

"Help!" he shouted. "Someone help me!"

Carina had raked her nails over the man's face but failed to damage his eyes. She switched tactics and gripped his neck, digging hard into his arteries. Moments later she felt him relax under her grip. She crawled out from underneath his large, heavy body.

One down, how many more to go? With disappointment Carina saw the man was unarmed. She stood up. There was a movement in the doorway. She turned, but before she could see what had caused it she felt the familiar and dreaded burst of a stun hitting her in the side.

The next time Carina woke, she felt tight restraints around her wrists and ankles. Those Sherrerr troops were getting smarter. But when she opened her eyes, she was surprised to see Bryce looking down at her.

"You're back with us?" He touched her hair affectionately. "Don't worry. You're safe. We're all safe."

"Huh?" Carina lifted her head. She was in the same place she'd been in before. Now that she had time to have a good look at it, she realized it was a medical bay. Darius lay in the next bed along from hers, asleep.

"They put me here to talk to you as soon as you woke up," said Bryce. "So you wouldn't go on another rampage. You already made yourself one enemy in that splicer you attacked."

"I don't give a shit about a Sherrerr splicer."

"He isn't a Sherrerr." Bryce grinned. "He's a mage."

"He's a *what*?" In order to see Darius better, Carina had lifted her head. It hit her pillow with a thump. "What the hell are you talking about?"

"That guy you tried to kill? He's a mage. They all call him a Healer, though. He was cleaning dried blood out of Darius' hair when you woke up and launched a full-scale assault on him." Bryce seemed to find what he was saying very funny.

"I.... Oh." Carina's mind was spinning. "Mages picked us up? How? Who are they? Bryce, what's going on?" Carina wondered if she'd been stunned in the head and was in a waking dream, or going mad.

"I don't know what's going on any more than you do," said Bryce. "Apart from what I've told you. They've said they'll explain everything soon. They also said they aren't going to hurt us. They're here to help."

***

Carina sat opposite the man she'd attacked, feeling slightly abashed about what she'd done. But the scratches she'd gouged on his face were gone and she guessed he must have Healed any further damage she'd done to him. From the look he was giving her, however, she guessed the harm she'd inflicted on his opinion of her would take longer to heal.

They were seated in a meeting room aboard the mages' ship, the *Haihu*.

Only Carina and her oldest sister had been invited to the meeting. Bryce, as a non-mage, had been excluded, and Carina's brothers and sisters were deemed too young to attend. Parthenia was making her hatred of Carina clear, as usual. She was sitting several seats away at the round table.

In all, four other mages were present, including an older woman, a young man, and a young woman. The Healer was a large, black-haired man. Carina suddenly caught her breath. She recognized him. He was one of the people she'd seen in her recurring dream. Parthenia was also looking at him curiously.

"Shall we get the introductions over with?" the older, white-haired woman asked. "I'm Eira, your captain. This is Ren, our navigator...." The young man nodded. "And Ione, our weapons officer." The redhead smiled. "I believe you've already met our Healer, Justin."

Justin did not smile.

"I'm Carina, and this is my sister, Parthenia."

"Thank you," Eira said. Her gaze lingered a long moment on Carina and her sister before she continued, "Some explanations are in order, from both sides. I'm hoping we can clear everything up today, or if not, over the course of our journey to Pirine. As you are both mages, I'm sure I don't need to explain the importance of never divulging to anyone what you are about to hear. It is for your siblings' safety as well as the safety of all mages that we keep our secrets close to our hearts. We can only know what is essential to us at each stage of our lives. If, stars forbid, one day you are forced to give up your knowledge, you will be less likely to imperil the future of our clan."

"I know," said Carina.

Parthenia echoed, "I understand."

"*You* are here, my dear," Eira said to Carina, "because you are close to the age where you could choose your match. You've been summoned to a Matching." Responding to Carina and Parthenia's puzzled looks, the captain went on, addressing Carina again, "You have been dreaming of coming to Pirine, haven't you?"

"I think I've been having dreams, yes. But they faded quickly when I woke up. I didn't know what they were about. I didn't know I was being called to go somewhere."

Eira sighed and traded glances with Justin. "Our Spirit Mage is very old and weak. Her Casting is not powerful any longer. We've heard similar reports from the young mages who have already arrived. To explain, every five galactic years, young men and women mages are Summoned by a Spirit Mage to a Matching. The event takes place over several months, and the young mages can get to know each other and perhaps choose a life partner. That is what your dreams have been about, Carina. I'm guessing you have no living relatives apart from your younger sisters and brothers?"

"That's right."

Eira looked pained. She continued, "If you had

an older mage in your life, he or she would have explained what the dreams meant."

"Right...," said Carina, "but Darius has been having the dreams too, I think. He's only six."

"He has been Summoned too," said Eira, "though for a different reason. Your brother is a Spirit Mage. Only one or two are born per generation. As I said, our current Spirit Mage who performs the Summons Cast is ancient. She has been Summoning your brother to her to take over from her. She must train him quickly before she dies.

"She has a stronger connection with your brother than other mages," said Eira. "That was how she knew he was coming to her, and how she also knew his path had been diverted. We set out to retrieve him. It was a dangerous expedition for us. We were forced to destroy the ship that was pursuing you, and that act will attract unwanted attention. But it was vital that we found your brother. Without a Spirit Mage our clan will die out."

"I've never heard of a Summon Cast," Parthenia interjected.

"That's because you can't do it," Justin replied. "Only Spirit Mages can."

"Excuse me," said Parthenia, looking at Justin, "but you look like someone I met once. Do you have a brother on Ostillon?"

"Ah, so it was you who wandered up to Jace's tower by the forest."

"It was!" Parthenia exclaimed. "My brother and I. So Jace was a mage all along? And I worked so hard to get away from him. If only I'd known, he could have helped us."

"He would have helped you however he could," said Justin, "and gladly. But by the time he realized what you were, you'd slipped away."

"I Cast Transport right in front of him," said Parthenia, laughing.

"It was quite a shock, from what he says," Justin said.

"That's the problem with all the secrecy, right?" said Ren. "We could be the friend of another mage all our lives and never know it."

"You met a mage on Ostillon?" Carina asked her sister.

Parthenia's expression turned sour and she replied without looking at Carina. "He was the ranger who helped me and Darius when we found our way out of the forest." She turned to Justin. "He's a good man. He saved us when we couldn't go any farther. The next time you see him, please thank him for me."

"You can thank him yourself," said Justin. "He'll be on Pirine soon, if he hasn't already arrived."

"He's coming to the Matching too?" Parthenia asked. "I thought it was just for young people."

Justin laughed, a deep-bellied chuckle. "He's only thirty-five. I'll tell him you said that. But Jace is coming to the Matching because—"

"Justin," Eira said sharply.

"Sorry," said the Healer, suddenly serious. "I was forgetting. Jace will be at the Matching too, Parthenia. He would have arrived earlier, but he was having problems leaving Ostillon due to the war."

"Is the war over now?" Carina asked.

"Yes, the Dirksens managed to repel the Sherrerr attack," said Eira.

"Probably with my other brother's help," said Carina.

"What?" asked Eira. "A mage is helping the Dirksens?"

"It's a long story," Carina replied.

"We have a lot to discuss," Eira said.

"You have another brother?" asked Ione. "You have a big family."

"He's my half-sibling, like Parthenia and all the others."

"So you two have different parents?" Eira said. "I'm surprised. You look so alike, it's obvious you're sisters. Do you mind telling me, do you share a mother?"

"We did," Carina replied. "Her name was Faye."

Eira's features clouded. "I feared it was so. I saw the resemblance right away but I hoped I was mistaken. She's dead, then?"

"She died a few months ago," said Carina.

"And Kris?"

"He passed on many years ago, before Parthenia was born."

Justin leaned forward and spread his arms on the table. "There are many sad tales to be told here, but let's save them for later. They're in the past now. You said you have another brother who you think is helping the Dirksens?"

"Ma had six children after me," said Carina. "Parthenia is the eldest. The second child is a boy called Castiel. My mother thought he wasn't a mage, but then around the time she died he developed mage powers. Unfortunately, he'd watched the lessons she had given the other children so he knew what he had to do in order to Cast."

"You say 'unfortunately?'" said Eira. "I'm guessing his behavior is not what you would expect from a mage."

"No, it isn't," said Parthenia. "Castiel is cruel and he lusts for power and control. He has to be stopped. I wanted to try to stop him, but Carina forced me to leave Ostillon." The venomous look she shot Carina left the room in an embarrassed silence.

"Well, that seems to be yet another subject we can explore more deeply another time," said Justin. "Are you in agreement over the nature of this young man?" he asked Carina.

"There's no doubt about it," she replied. "I'm not sure why he is as he is. Perhaps he takes after his father, or perhaps growing up without mage ability in a family of mages has warped him, but Castiel is evil."

Eira's somber expression deepened.

"I'm so glad you found us," said Parthenia. "Maybe we can work together to defeat my brother?"

"We certainly need to address that question," said Eira. "I'm not sure what the answer is."

"I'm worried that Castiel and the Dirksens may follow us," said Carina. "I think the ship you attacked when you found us belonged to that clan."

"It did," Justin said. "We had a rather terse exchange of comms. The ship's captain stated you were escaped prisoners of war. We declined to believe them." He smiled grimly.

"But when the Dirksens don't hear anything from their ship they'll send out another to find out what happened to it. Then they'll pick up your trace and follow it the same as they followed ours."

"No, they won't," said Eira. "Don't worry, Ren has Cast Obscure on our trail and will continue to do so. It's extremely unlikely they would discover our path, and if they do, they would also need to search all of Pirine to find us."

Carina wasn't entirely reassured by Eira's words, but she bowed to the older woman's long experience. She also had more questions she was urged to ask. "Can you tell me more about my mother and father? I grew up without them. My Nai Nai brought me up. I only met my mother again not long before she died."

"I would love to," Eira replied. "I propose that we bring the meeting to a close first, however. I think we've touched on all the important topics for today. Thank you for what you've told us. Remember, do not tell anyone else anything we've discussed here. Your non-mage friend and your brothers and sisters will naturally make some guesses about what's happening, but it's really best for everyone that they know as little as possible for certain."

Carina imagined it would be hard to not tell Bryce why they were going to Pirine, how the mages had found them, or answer any other mysteries that had been cleared up for her. But he probably wouldn't press her for answers. He understood the need for secrecy.

The fact that she was supposed to attend this

'Matching' troubled her more. She wasn't of a mind to match to anyone.

People were leaving the meeting room. Justin had risen from his seat and was walking past Carina when he halted and she felt a heavy hand on her shoulder. When she looked up at him, he held out his other hand. Somewhat bewildered, she grasped it and they shook.

"There are not many who have made me cry for help," he said, a twinkle in the depths of his deep-set eyes.

Carina said, "I'm sorry. I hope I didn't hurt you."

"Nothing a little Casting couldn't fix." He released his grip and walked out.

***

Carina was pleased to see her brothers and sisters put on weight and lose their worry lines as the days passed while the *Haihu* took them to Pirine. Bryce also relaxed and cheered up considerably as the journey wore on. As Carina had predicted, he didn't push her for information.

Eira spent some time reminiscing with Carina about her mother and father. It turned out that she'd gotten to know them at a Matching long ago, when Carina's parents had met. Eira told Carina what she recalled, mainly about how much in love her parents had seemed. That was one reason Eira remembered them so well.

Carina listened hungrily as Eira spoke of her mother. She wanted to overlay her final memories of the poor woman, ravaged with disease and long years of cruelty, with mental images of her as a young, happy, innocent young person in the first flush of love.

When Eira told Carina about her father, she built memories of a man she had all but forgotten. She wished so much that mage lore didn't prohibit keeping images of loved ones. She could barely remember Ba's face.

Carina didn't tell Darius anything about what lay ahead of him on Pirine, partly because she didn't have much of an idea what Eira's mention of 'training' actually meant. The captain had said she couldn't tell her any more. The prospect worried Carina. Darius was only six years old. He might be a Spirit Mage but he was still only a little boy, much too young to have the responsibility of the future of mages on his shoulders.

Finally, the day came when they arrived at Pirine's star system. Eira announced the fact when she came into the small mess one morning.

Oriana clapped her hands. "Wonderful! I can finally have a proper bath. And real food...though the ship's food is also nice," she added, remembering her manners.

"We're all looking forward to real food," said Eira kindly. "But I'm afraid a bath won't be possible where we're going. I'll explain to you what happens next. We have to hide the *Haihu* at the edge of the system, then we take a shuttle in."

"How come we don't go straight to Pirine?" Ferne asked. "I thought it was a mage planet."

"There are no mage planets, Ferne," said Eira. "Not any longer. Whenever mages settled a new planet, non-mages would come along and drive them out, until finally they had to hide within non-mage populations. Pirine is no exception, though the people there are more tolerant and less suspicious of outsiders than most. We must keep our abilities secret on Pirine the same as everywhere. However, at the place we're going, everyone is a mage. It's a temporary encampment. After we arrive there, I must ask you not to question anyone about where they're from, or even ask their names if they do not volunteer them."

"How long will we be staying?" asked Darius.

"That isn't clear yet," Eira replied. "We'll be transferring to the shuttle in about an hour. Make sure you're ready."

The *Haihu*'s shuttle was a small silver oblong that barely fit everyone. Carina was quiet as they sped through the system toward the distant sun. So much had happened in the previous weeks. They had been in so much danger, but they had all survived relatively unscathed. Bryce, who was sitting next to her, took her hand. She smiled, but then an idea struck her. Would the mages at the encampment accept Bryce and Nahla?

Darius was sitting on Parthenia's lap because there weren't enough seats for everyone. He piped up, rather proudly, "Eira, do you want me to Cloak the ship?"

"What's that?" asked Justin.

Carina explained about Darius' special Cast, and Eira said, "Yes, we would like that very much indeed. The Pirine authorities aren't tight on security but there's no point in taking risks we can avoid."

Two hours later, the shuttle touched down. It was a relief to leave the cramped ship. When Carina walked out the exit ramp, she was greeted by a familiar sight. They had landed in the middle of a grassy plain that stretched out in all directions.

Carina had never been to Pirine in her life, but she realized she'd visited the planet many times in her dreams.

"Please move forward," said Eira from behind. "You're blocking the exit. We must hide the shuttle as soon as we can."

Carina walked out into the hot, dry atmosphere of Pirine. It was around midday, and the air was exactly as she'd dreamed it: full of the scent of wildflowers and the sound of insects.

"But where are we going to sleep?" asked Oriana.

"Over there," said Justin, pointing behind the shuttle.

Carina turned and saw a collection of tents in the distance.

"Ugh," said Oriana, "we're going to sleep in those?!"

"Oh shut up," said Ferne. "It'll be great."

They headed out toward the campsite, along a lightly worn path through the tall grass. A sound from behind her made Carina turn, and she was just in time to see the shuttle disappearing beneath a shelter disguised as a pile of boulders.

Before they had crossed half the distance, another sight familiar to Carina appeared. A very old woman hobbled from out of the shadow of a tent. It was the woman from Carina's dreams, who she now remembered clear as day, right down to the woman's piercing stare. Though she was almost bent double, she moved at a surprising speed as she closed the distance between them.

She suddenly paused and lifted one hand to shade her eyes while the other remained on her stick. "Darius," she called, her voice thin and feeble. "Darius! I can see you. Come here, my sweet boy."

Darius turned questioning eyes to Carina. She didn't know what to say. The old woman, who she guessed was the Spirit Mage, clearly recognized Darius. "Should I go, Carina?"

"I guess so."

Her brother walked a little faster than the group so that he was soon farther ahead. He met with the Spirit Mage about half a minute before the rest of them caught up to him. The mage had one bony arm across Darius' shoulders and was leaning her ancient face close to his youthful one. Her expression seemed to convey joy, but Carina also thought she saw a horrible glint of avarice in the old woman's eyes.

Darius looked fearful.

CHAPTER SIXTEEN

Winter had arrived quickly at the mountain castle, and the rooms had grown even colder. As Castiel's servant, who he'd learned was called Vera, left his bed, he told her to maintain a constant fire for him. The innuendo of his request wasn't lost on him, and he smirked as she dressed herself.

When his servant went out and closed the door, however, his smile faded. The wonder and pleasure he'd experienced when she'd offered herself to him so readily a few weeks previously had quickly palled. He'd discovered that the fruit given freely held no sweetness.

At the same time, his desire for Sable Dirksen had escalated. While Vera was in his bed, Castiel imagined she was Sable. He even used the clan leader's name, and he acted out the degradations and perversions he planned using on her when she became his. When that might happen was still uncertain, but he believed he edged closer toward the goal every day.

Castiel threw back the covers and climbed out

of bed. Despite the heating system the Dirksens had installed and the crackling fire in the grate, he shivered. The clammy chill never went away in the mountain castle abode. Castiel pulled on his pants and put on a shirt, and then the thick, padded jacket he'd ordered to be made. His clothes felt tight. He guessed he'd done some growing. His arms and chest certainly seemed more muscular.

He faced the mirror and checked out his appearance. His beard nearly covered most of his jaw and his face had lost some of its roundness. He imagined he must look similar to his father when he was young. All the more fitting that he should achieve Father's ambition for him. What a pity he would not be around to witness it. He would have liked to make the old man proud.

It was nearly time for dinner. Castiel left his room to go downstairs to the great hall. He didn't care about punctuality, but these days dinnertime was about the only time of the day when he could reliably speak to Sable. Most days she was gone from the castle, though she never told him where she went.

He walked down the steps, remembering that horrible period when Sable had set him to helping with the restoration of the capital. How demeaning that had been. He should have refused her request, or made his protest earlier. His most recent task of trying to extract information from the Sherrerr spy who had given away information about Ostillon had been far more enjoyable.

He hadn't managed to find out anything useful, he had to admit, but he had had fun trying.

When Castiel strutted into the hall, he was

surprised by the sight of a guest for dinner. Commander Kee had joined them. Castiel hadn't seen the man since his first day at the castle, when he'd made the unfortunate error of killing Tremoille. He wondered what had happened to Calvaley. He hadn't heard anything about the old man.

"Commander Kee," said Castiel in a statesman-like manner as he arrived at the dining table, "you're with us again. Do you have something important to report?"

Kee gave him a sardonic look, and Castiel noticed the man failed to stand up and salute him.

"Now then, Castiel," said a voice. Sable stood in the doorway. "Don't tempt the commander into giving away secrets." She entered the hall, looking magnificent. She was wearing a floor-length, high-necked gown made of a rich, thick, black fabric. Castiel had expected a woman of her wealth and status to wear expensive jewelry, like the kind his father had given his mother, but as always Sable wore none. Somehow the absence of decoration seemed to make her appear more impressive.

Kee pushed back his chair, stood, and saluted as she approached the table. Castiel scowled and pulled out a chair, deliberately scraping the legs across the stone floor. He threw himself into his seat. How dare Sable imply he was not allowed to hear Dirksen 'secrets.' How much longer would he be treated as an outsider? Sable and Kee ignored his petulance and sat down.

"Thank you for joining us, Commander," said Sable. "I know you must be tired after your flight."

"It's always a pleasure to attend you, ma'am."

"I read over your report just now, but I'd also like to hear it in your own words. That was why I requested your presence tonight."

"Ah...." Kee's gaze flicked to Castiel.

"You can speak freely in front of Castiel. This business concerns him."

Castiel perked up. "I'm all ears." He took a sip of wine. Over his weeks at Sable's castle, he'd become more accustomed to the drink and could now tolerate three or four glasses before becoming unsteady. He'd been careful not to repeat the shameful event of his first taste of alcohol.

"In that case," said Kee, "as I wrote, ma'am, we confirmed the debris we found was from the *Torpille*, the destroyer we sent in pursuit of the mage children. We were unable to establish the cause of the ship's destruction. We found no impact site. It was as if the ship exploded from within."

"They probably Cast Fire into the ship's fuel tanks," said Castiel with a tone that he hoped made him appear knowledgeable. "That was how Carina and the others destroyed your shipyard. They knew where the tanks were, you see."

"I thought you said it was *you* who destroyed our shipyard?" said Sable.

"Oh, er," Castiel said, blood heating his cheeks. "That was what I meant."

"Continue, Kee."

"I'm not convinced it was the mage children who destroyed the *Torpille*. It might have been another ship. We found the shuttle, adrift but empty, without any bodies inside. That made little sense to me. The only explanation that accounted for all the evidence was that the *Torpille* picked up the mages but then was destroyed by an unknown force. Would the mage children commit an act of self-destruction? It seemed unlikely.

"So we searched. That was the cause of our delay, ma'am. We were combing the territory for any signs of a trace from a third ship. Luckily for us the area is rarely frequented. We finally picked up some patchy signs a week's travel from the site of the *Torpille's* destruction. They led in the direction of a planetary system with a single inhabited planet called Pirine."

"I looked up Pirine when I saw your report," said Sable. "The planet doesn't seem to have any significance. I don't understand why a ship from there would travel out to the shuttle to collect the children. Perhaps Castiel can shed some light? Do you remember hearing anyone in your family refer to that planet?"

Castiel trawled his memory. "No, I don't. I think it's unlikely anyone did. We never used to talk about other planets. Father didn't place much emphasis on galactic topography in our education."

"Could the ship have been a Sherrerr vessel?" Sable asked Kee.

"Impossible to say yet, ma'am."

"Pirine has never demonstrated sufficient potential for either us or the Sherrerrs to take control of it," Sable said. "The economy is almost entirely agrarian due to the scarcity of natural resources. The only explanation for what you observed that makes sense to me is that a portion of the Sherrerr fleet fled there after their failed attempt to take Ostillon. Did you find any evidence that might support that scenario, Kee?"

"We didn't approach the planet closely, but from what we could tell the evidence of space traffic seemed normal for a planet of Pirine's low economic and political importance. But the trace we were following disappeared at the system's edge. Consequently, we weren't able to ascertain where the ship landed, if in fact it ended up on Pirine itself."

"Disappearing traces," said Sable. "That sounds like mage work. You mean these people could be hiding out on an uninhabited planet or moon somewhere in the system?"

"A moon would be the only possibility. The other planets are high-gravity or gaseous giants, unfit for human life."

"Hmmm. Well, it seems we have narrowed down the possibilities considerably. Thank you for your excellent work, Kee. Now we have to act. What do you think we should do, Castiel?"

Jerked from reverie, Castiel splashed wine on himself. He put down his glass and picked up a napkin. As he dabbed at himself, disconcerted, he replied, "We should travel to Pirine and find my brothers and sisters. As you said, Sable, as long as they aren't working for us they're a liability. We can't allow the Sherrerrs to have them."

"They would be even less of a liability if we killed them," said Sable. "What do you think about that?"

"Killed them?" The idea appealed. He'd always imagined himself controlling his siblings in the same way as Father had. As well as all the things he could do with their help, it would be payback for years of living as a second-class member of his own family.

Yet Sable had a point. With no other mages around, his own abilities would become rarer and more precious. He would have no competition, no one to make him look lesser.

The thought of ending the lives of the siblings he'd grown up with gave him a strange sensation. Was this how guilt felt? Never mind. He would soon get over it. "It might be difficult to kill them due to their abilities, especially my half-sister, Carina. She trained as a merc. But though they can Cast, they're still human and can be killed the same ways."

Kee had been watching Castiel as he spoke. At this last sentence he turned his head away in disgust. Sable's expression remained enigmatic. Castiel recalled her statement the first time he'd met her, that she couldn't stand disloyalty. Had he said the wrong thing? It couldn't be helped. If his siblings' deaths were necessary for his elevation to power, so be it. He wouldn't shed a tear for any of them, least of all Carina.

"Very well," said Sable. "What's clear is that we must prepare a small fleet to fly to Pirine. I want to find these mages before they become a threat. If we can't put them to work for us, we'll put them out of action, permanently. How long will it take for you to equip a cruiser?"

"The repairs on the *Elsinore* are nearly complete, ma'am," said Kee. "I would only need another two days to make her ready."

"Good. We can work out the details later.

Castiel, are you excited to finally have something to get your teeth into?"

"Me? You mean I'm going too?"

"Of course. Who better to defeat mages than another mage?"

"Great!" Castiel exclaimed. Then he reasserted his composure. "That's excellent news. I'll look forward to it."

***

Despite his intention to restrain himself, Castiel drank too much that evening. He was overjoyed that Sable was finally including him in an important, noteworthy task. While she and Kee chatted about what troops to assign finding and capturing or killing his siblings and other plans, Castiel ran through many scenarios in his mind, each involving a moment of supreme triumph.

He would either decisively Repulse his brothers and sisters' Casts, resulting in their capture, or he would order soldiers to shoot them. Or perhaps he would trick them into a trap and lock them up, depriving them of their elixir so they were weak and helpless.

The last scenario triggered a realization: he hadn't brought his elixir with him to the dining table. Not long after he'd arrived at the castle, he'd told Sable he needed something more convenient and portable than his glass bottle in which to carry the liquid essential to Casting. She'd suggested he commission an Ostillonian craftsman to create something. Castiel had found a metalworker who had made him an ornate canister inscribed with his initials. Usually, he went everywhere with it, but that evening he didn't have it with him.

The warmth the alcohol had given him drained away in a moment and was replaced by a chill. Castiel felt naked, and Sable and Kee, who were chatting animatedly about ship-to-ground weapons, seemed suddenly dark and distant. Without his elixir, he was nothing and nobody. Sable could kick him out of the castle and tell one of her servants to break his back on a rock, and there would be nothing he could do about it.

"Are you feeling unwell?" Sable asked him, noticing the change in his features.

"Maybe ma'am should ask someone to bring a bucket," Kee quipped.

Castiel swallowed. "I'm all right. I'm just tired. I think I'll go to bed now."

"Good night, then," said Sable, immediately returning her attention to Kee.

Castiel stood up, the backs of his knees pushing away his chair. He wavered and grabbed the tabletop for support. Kee rolled his eyes. Castiel walked off unsteadily. He had to get to his elixir. He'd left it in his room. He only needed to feel the reassuring touch of the cold metal canister. He vowed never to be without it again.

He took the elevator even though his room was on the next floor. It was faster and he didn't trust himself on the steps. To fall down would be the height of embarrassment. When the elevator doors opened, he leaned on one edge for support as he stepped out into the corridor.

As soon as he reached his room Castiel went straight to the bedside drawer where he kept the canister. He pulled it open and blinked for a few moments as he took in what he saw. Horror struck him. The drawer was empty! He pulled out the one below it and the third one. Then he pulled out all the drawers and scrabbled around the empty frame. He pulled the furniture away from the wall and threw it across the room. Where could his elixir be? He was certain he'd put the canister in its usual place before Vera had come to pay him her daily visit.

Castiel searched his room, stripping the covers from his bed, tossing the pillows onto the floor. He peered underneath the bed, and then dragged it away from the wall. He remembered the clothing chest in the corner of the room. Of course! He must have put the elixir in there by accident. But when he lifted the lid and hauled out all the clothes, the canister wasn't inside. Where could it be?

Castiel grabbed his hair in frustration. He had to find the precious liquid. Everything depended on it. If it wasn't in his room it had to be because someone had stolen it. Perhaps Vera was the thief. The stupid girl was infatuated with him. She'd taken it in order to have something of his. Or perhaps another servant had taken it, imagining they could sell the canister for a good price.

That had to be the answer. One of the servants had taken it. He would have to find out who it was and demand that Sable fire them—after punishing them heavily.

He marched out of his room, anger driving away the effects of his excessive drinking. He went down the stairs and rushed into the great hall. "One of your servants has stolen my elixir," he blurted.

Kee was standing and pushing in his chair. Sable was draining her glass. Both turned to Castiel, their eyes widening at his outburst.

"I demand that all the servants' quarters are searched until it's found. And the thief must be punished severely."

"Your elixir?" asked Kee. "Do you mean this?" He picked up Castiel's canister from the tabletop.

It had been there all along! Castiel realized he must have put it down somewhere he couldn't see it and, in his drunken state, he'd assumed he'd forgotten it.

Castiel wished he could undo his outburst. He wished he could wind time back by one minute. But he couldn't.

"Yes," he said quietly, "that's it."

Kee maintained a sardonic gaze on Castiel as he crossed the hall. The commander held the canister out at arm's length, waiting for Castiel to take it from him. When the container changed hands, Castiel returned to the staircase, feeling Sable and Kee watching him the entire way. They were silent, but after he'd climbed a few steps and was out of their sight, Sable's laughter peeled out and was quickly joined by Kee's loud, deep chuckles.

Castiel opened the door to his room and surveyed the mess he'd created. He was furious. He hated Sable and Kee for laughing at his mistake. He hated that he'd done something so stupid.

One thing that was clear, he wasn't going to sleep in the disarray caused by his frantic search. He went to his interface and called the servants' quarters, demanding that Vera come up to his room instantly and tidy it up.

He flung himself onto his bed. He would take out his anger on the girl when she arrived. A minute later there was a knock at the door and it opened. The servant panting outside wasn't Vera but another young girl.

Castiel sat up in surprise. "Where's Vera?"

"I don't know, sir," the girl replied, catching her breath after running to his room. "I was told I am to be your room servant from now on. My name is —"

"I don't give a shit what your name is. I want to know what...." Did he really want to know what had happened to Vera? Not at all. Or at least, not if this girl could meet his needs in the same way. She was certainly as pretty as Vera had been.

"I want you to tidy up this mess," he said, "but that isn't all. Come over here."

The girl took quick steps across the room until she was only a few feet from his side.

"Take off your clothes."

To Castiel's surprise, the girl complied with his instructions without a moment's hesitation. Castiel's eyes widened. It was so easy! Vera hadn't been a fluke. It was much easier than he'd been led to believe in stories he'd read and dramas he'd watched. But maybe it wasn't so remarkable. After all, he was an important member of the Dirksen household. Of course the girl would do whatever he wanted. Perhaps what was happening was normal in rich and powerful clans.

Come to think of it, Castiel remembered seeing his father caressing the female servants in the mansion on Ithiya.

So this was normal. If only he'd realized earlier, he could have had so much more fun.

The girl was naked.

"Well, what are you waiting for?" Castiel barked. "Get on the bed." His former anger over his embarrassing mistake returned. He would work it out of his system on this girl. She would soon perform her service in as much discomfort and pain as he could inflict, and afterward he would watch as she tidied up his room.

He used the servant roughly, yet though she didn't enjoy it, she didn't seem to mind too much. Castiel wondered if she'd been beaten frequently at home and so she'd become insensitive to pain.

When he was finished, he pushed her away from him. "Get dressed—no, wait. Pick up in here before putting your clothes on. Then you can leave."

"Yes, sir." The girl climbed off the bed and Castiel let his gaze linger on her welts and developing bruises. He had exhausted himself. He could have performed more interesting feats by Casting, but it would not have been as satisfying or cathartic. Expending his strength was much better. His drunkenness had worn off too and he felt the beginnings of a headache. When the girl was gone, he would Heal himself before he slept.

His eyelids drooping, Castiel watched the servant as she folded the clothes scattered about the floor and carefully laid them inside the chest in the corner. Was she smiling to herself? It seemed she was. Castiel's eyelids lifted and he pulled himself back from the brink of sleep.

Why was the girl smiling? Was she a masochist? Had she enjoyed all that he'd done to her? He felt cheated. What he'd done was for his pleasure, not hers. If she liked it, that took away most of the point of the exercise.

Castiel thought back to Vera. She also hadn't seemed to particularly mind what he did to her, no matter how brutal he'd been. It was a strange coincidence that the two servants had reacted in the same way.

It was too much of a coincidence. Castiel wasn't as experienced as he hoped to become, but even he knew that most women didn't like being ill-treated in that way. He'd seen his mother shrink from his father's approach often enough to know that.

So, why— He sat bolt upright. "You." He pointed at her, though he couldn't possibly mean anyone else. "Why are you here?"

"I'm your room servant, sir."

He was out of bed in an instant and by her side. He grabbed a fistful of the girl's hair and wrenched it, twisting her neck and bending her head almost to the floor. "Why are you really here?"

"Owww, please, sir! Please, let go!" She fell to her knees.

"Ha, you don't like it so much now, do you? Not now there's no point to it? Not now you aren't exciting me." Castiel had a vision of throwing the girl down and stomping on her face until she told him the answer. But Sable Dirksen had probably threatened even worse punishments.

Sable was no mage, however. She couldn't stop him from finding out the truth, though he already knew it. He just wanted to hear it from the girl's lips.

"Stay there," Castiel said. In three strides he was across the room and taking his elixir canister from the drawer. He sipped the liquid, closed his eyes, and Cast Enthrall. He opened his eyes. The girl's stare was blank when he returned to her.

"You, why were you sent here?"

"I am your room—"

He kicked her. "What was the other reason you were sent here?"

"I am to allow you to use me, sir."

"And why is that?" Castiel's hands were clenching into fists.

"So that I may become pregnant, sir. If I give birth to a live child sired by you, my family will be richly rewarded."

He let out a roar and punched the girl in the face.

"And Vera? She is pregnant? That's why you replaced her?"

"Yes, sir."

Castiel knocked the girl down. She lay where she fell, blood oozing from her nose. Castiel began to kick her, over and over.

Sable Dirksen had been tricking him the whole time. After he'd told her that magehood was passed on from parent to child, she'd hatched a plan to force him to sire children for her. More mages who would be entirely under her control.

Damn her! Damn Sable Dirksen and all her schemes. He would not forget her treachery and deceit. Not for a very long time.

CHAPTER SEVENTEEN

When Carina and her siblings had arrived at the Matching, they carried little more with them than the clothes on their backs. Not long after they walked into the camp, however, with Eira, Justin, and the rest of the crew of the *Haihu*, they had food, somewhere to sleep, and the warmest welcome Carina had ever known.

It had taken her days to become accustomed to the idea that she no longer had to hide what she was from strangers, because everyone she met was the same as her. She had never known a time when she had not been forced to keep her abilities secret, with the threat of torture, slavery, or death hanging over her. The new sense of freedom was dizzying, and Carina's brothers and sisters seemed to feel the same. After a childhood spent living under the domination of their father in a household full of pain, and long months of hiding and running, they could finally relax and be themselves.

The boys and girls had become more childlike, playing endlessly in the long grass of the prairie. Even Parthenia had joined in their games of tag or hide-and-go-seek. Over the days they had grown fatter and the color returned to their faces.

While the children played, Carina had spent time wandering around the camp. She discovered that there was no formal structure to the Matching. Over the course of months, young mages would arrive, spend as much time at the camp as they wanted, and then leave at a time of their choosing. Some left with partners they had met, others had the locations of new friends memorized in order to arrange later meetings. A few left without either of these things, but it seemed not unhappily. Perhaps they would return for the next Matching, or perhaps they were content to remain single.

The young mages passed their days meeting and talking with others, over meals or drinks. Some had brought musical instruments with them and gave performances, others sang, recited poetry, or put on plays. Some taught skills like cooking and crafting.

Carina's memory of her dreams became stronger now that she was actually at the place she'd dreamed about, and the camp retained a dreamlike quality for her. She almost could not believe it was real. Was it because it felt too good to be true, and if she truly believed in it, the place might suddenly vanish in a puff of smoke?

As if to keep her anchored in the more familiar, harsh world outside the Matching, two aspects of the camp marred her experience. The first was that she did not fit in. The young mages she met had clearly been raised in loving families and if they had experienced hardship it was only of the economical kind. The second problem Carina had with the camp was how Darius' days were spent.

While his brothers and sisters played, he spent most of his time with the Spirit Mage. When he returned to their tent after a long day of training with the old woman, he was often too tired to play and he would fall asleep soon after dinner.

Darius said he was helping the Spirit Mage, whose name was Magda, with her Summoning, and she had begun to teach him some things that only Spirit Mages could do. Carina's unease about the situation increased but she wasn't sure what to do about it. One thing that particularly saddened her was that Darius was asleep in the evenings when the Spirit Mage told her stories, though Carina guessed that Darius would eventually know all the stories himself.

It turned out that one of Magda's roles was to function as the repository for the oral history of the clan. Every night, a couple of hours after the sun had set, someone would build a large fire at the center of the encampment, and the Spirit Mage would sit beside it and tell a story from the mages' ancient past. She told a different story every night, and would often say she knew more stories than she could tell at one Matching.

Though Carina disliked the way the old woman had monopolized Darius, she would often attend these story tellings. Parthenia would come to listen to the stories too, but Carina knew better than to attempt to sit with her sister. When she'd tried, Parthenia had gotten up and walked away, drawing the curious stares of others. So instead, Carina usually found a space at the edge of the crowd far from the fire and sat on a blanket that had been spread over the damp, flattened grass. She would cover her shoulders with another blanket for warmth, and listen.

One evening the Spirit Mage told a very old story from the time the mages departed their home planet, Earth. Carina's attention increased in focus when she understood what the subject was to be. She had never given up her dream of returning to Earth one day.

"At that time, most of Earth's population was living in a country called Antarctica," said Magda, "which spanned the southern pole. The equatorial regions were desert wastelands, too hot for human survival, and the land masses in between were tropical wildernesses, disease-ridden, and the sites of frequent hurricanes, tornadoes, and floods. Some communities survived in the high mountains, and the mage clan was one of these.

"Earth had not always been in this state, with so few areas suitable for human habitation. Humanity had lived and thrived all over the globe for hundreds of thousands of years. But successive decades of poor management of the planet had driven its systems to extremes that were not compatible with human life in most areas.

"The planetary government's proposed solution to this crisis was to approach the mage clan and insist that they use their special abilities to fix the damage and return Earth to its previous, livable state. No amount of explanation would convince the government that this was a task that was entirely beyond mages. Or perhaps the government did not want to hear. Perhaps all it needed was a scapegoat, for its next step was to announce to the world's media that the mage clan had refused to aid humankind, that it was waiting for non-mages to die out. Then mages would make Earth into a paradise that only they could enjoy.

"The government employed technology that put the words into the mouths of the Mage Council on vids and holos. Try as they might to deny the lies, the mages were not believed. Perhaps the rest of the population wanted to believe the deceit, which made them easy to convince. By that time, mages had long been feared and hated. Rumors abounded of what kind of people they were and how they lived in their secret mountain castles, most of which were untrue. The mages were so divorced from regular human life, they rarely attempted to correct what was said about them.

"Due to the government's propaganda as it sought to deflect the blame for its failings, resentment against mages grew ever stronger. The clan came to the decision that remaining on Earth was simply too dangerous. If they did not leave, one day their mountain abodes would be attacked and they would be murdered or enslaved. The engine that permitted interstellar space travel had been invented, and the mages determined that they would be among the first to abandon Earth for the stars.

"It took them longer than two Earth years to construct their colony ship, but eventually the day came when they were to board the vessel and depart their home forever. A few of the clan did not want to leave. Many sad goodbyes were said, and then the thousands began to Transport to the launch site.

"Though the construction of the ship had taken place in great secrecy, word had gotten out to the general populace that the mages were departing Earth. The first mages Transporting into the site found a scene of bloody murder and destruction. People who had hated mages all their lives also did not want them to leave. They demanded that the clan remain on Earth and help the rest of humankind. They said it was their duty and responsibility.

"So these non-mages had tried to prevent the ship from leaving by killing those who guarded it. They were also trying to sabotage the engines when the colonists arrived. A battle ensued, and though the mages Transported many of those who were trying to prevent them from leaving the scene, for the first time they were forced to kill in order to protect themselves. They won the battle, and they knew their time on Earth was done.

"Thus it was, with sorrow and shame our ancestors departed their home, never to return."

The Spirit Mage fell silent. The story was over. After the mage had taken a drink and a few moments to gather her thoughts, she would begin another. The evening was growing late, and possibly the next story she told would be the last that night.

Parts of this story of leaving Earth were new to Carina. Ma had told her that mages had left due to persecution, but she hadn't given her the details about the state of the planet. Carina wondered if her ambition to return to Earth was foolish. She might go to a massive effort to arrive at the home planet only to find a barren wilderness.

As Carina was contemplating this idea, a tall figure approached out of the darkness where the light from the fire didn't reach. The man was tall and broad and at first Carina thought it was Justin who had come to listen, but then she saw that the man's beard was shorter.

Carina peered over at the man and was surprised to see him sit down next to Parthenia. The two talked quietly while the Spirit Mage began her next story. Carina guessed the newcomer was Justin's brother, the ranger at the tower on Ostillon.

Carina did not listen to the new story. Disappointment tormented her. The Spirit Mage's story seemed to have sucked away Carina's hopes for a future of safety and happiness far from that galactic sector in the mages' former home. She realized that she had been listening to Magda's stories so avidly because she'd been hoping to hear information that would give clues to Earth's location. But the Spirit Mage's tale had driven home the fact that her clan had been intent on getting as far from Earth as they could, not returning there. In the story that had been passed down no galactic coordinates were mentioned.

Yet there was the Map, which she had drawn thousands of times over as a child and which she still recalled every time she meditated. Someone in the distant past of mages had wanted Earth's location to be remembered, perhaps long after its galactic coordinates had become obsolete and meaningless.

Carina pondered the problem, withdrawing into herself, until before she knew it the Spirit Mage's final story was over and the crowd was breaking up to go to bed. She stood and shook out her legs to ease their stiffness after sitting for so long. Parthenia and the ranger remained seated together and talking. Carina walked over to the pair.

The ranger noticed her approaching and rose to his feet, holding out his hand. "Carina, my name is Jace. It's nice to meet you again."

Parthenia turned her face away.

Carina shook the ranger's hand, somewhat perplexed. "Again? Have we already met?"

"Yes, though only briefly, before you and your brothers and sisters disappeared."

"Huh?" Carina wondered what he meant. Then the penny dropped and her eyes widened. "Of course. How stupid of me. That was you at the forest on Ostillon."

"It was. I was walking alone after dark, laying low and waiting for the hostilities between the Sherrerrs and Dirksens to blow over so I could leave the planet and come here, when I spotted a fire in among the trees. I made my way over, wondering who could be there, so far from civilization. I saw your shelter and went over for a closer look.

"Imagine my surprise when the sleepers in the shelter began to disappear before my eyes. It didn't take me long to realize that you were mages

Transporting yourselves away, afraid of discovery. And then I also guessed that you must have something to do with the two mage children I had helped weeks previously, one of whom I've finally found again." He smiled at Parthenia, but she continued to hold her face averted.

Jace frowned in confusion.

"It's okay," said Carina. "It isn't you Parthenia is mad at, it's me." She took a breath and let it out in a sigh, ashamed of what she was about to admit. "I cast Enthrall on her to force her to leave Ostillon."

"You...?" asked Jace, eyes widening. "That was...." He paused, too polite to state his opinion.

"A terrible thing to do," said Carina. "I know, and I hated to do it, but I didn't want Parthenia to die." She paused again, and then her guilt and unhappiness regarding her relationship with her sister overcame her and words flooded from her mouth without hindrance.

"She means so much to me. Her help was invaluable when we escaped the Sherrerrs. I could never have done it without her, and after that she kept our brothers and sister safe in dangerous, difficult circumstances. She's quick-thinking, resourceful, and smart, and I love her. I couldn't leave her on Ostillon, even if it meant taking away her free will. I'm sorry for it, but I don't regret it. I would do the same again because I can't bear to lose her, not after losing Ma."

Carina hadn't been aware what she was going to say before she said it. Yet she'd meant it all and was glad she'd had the opportunity to tell her sister how she felt.

Parthenia's head remained turned away, but

Carina sensed a small change in her, as if her sister had been affected by what she'd said.

"I think I understand what happened," said Jace. "You faced a hard choice."

"I didn't have a good option to pick."

"But I don't know that staying on Ostillon was as dangerous as you think," said Jace. "As long as you avoided the populated areas you should have been fairly safe. I myself only had to wait until regular space travel was allowed again before I could leave."

"Oh, don't you know about our brother, Castiel?" asked Parthenia.

"No, I haven't heard that name. I only just arrived."

"That's a long story," said Carina, "and a discussion we need to have with Magda, Justin, and anyone else who's in charge here. But the short version is, our brother is a Dark Mage, and he's helping the Dirksens."

"A Dark Mage?" asked Jace. "That is bad news. So that was why you didn't want to leave your sister on Ostillon? It makes more sense now. Dark Mages are difficult to defeat, even for many mages working together. You could not have accomplished that alone, Parthenia."

"But we must try," she said. "We can't allow Castiel to do whatever he wants. He's cruel and vicious. He'll cause untold suffering."

"You mean like the untold suffering that non-mages have caused us over the millenia?" asked Carina. "Honestly, the more I think about it, the less certain I am that we should do anything about Castiel. Hearing the Spirit Mage's story has made me consider changing my mind. Think about it, Parthenia. The Sherrerrs knew what your father was doing, and they didn't do anything to stop him. They *chose* not to do anything, because you were all useful to them.

"Why should we help humankind when they've never helped us? We haven't done anything to deserve the persecution we've suffered. I know I said I would go back to Ostillon to tackle Castiel, but now I'm not so sure."

"How can you say that?" Parthenia exclaimed. "Castiel deserves to be punished for everything he's done. He deserves to be locked away and prevented from harming anyone. And we're the only ones who can defeat him."

"I don't know about that either," Carina said. "Your father did a good job of controlling his mage wife and offspring. Maybe Castiel isn't as invincible as you think. Maybe the Dirksens already have him under their control. Even now he could be suffering torture to force him to do their bidding. I'm sorry, Parthenia. I'm not sure this is our fight."

Jace said, "One thing is certain, this subject needs further discussion, but not tonight. Let me speak with my brother and the Spirit Mage. What to do about a Dark Mage in our midst is a decision that will impact us all."

CHAPTER EIGHTEEN

As the Dirksen fleet was prepared to set out for Pirine, Castiel was careful not to let Sable know he was aware of her plans to trick him into siring children. When the new girl came to his room, he Enthralled her and made her believe that she had slept with him, and he remembered to rough her up a little too to make the lie seem convincing. Sable Dirksen might have gotten one child out of him but she would not get any more.

Castiel's mind had ranged across the various ways he might get his revenge on Sable Dirksen. He'd imagined killing her in a range of painful ways. He'd imagined imprisoning her and forcing her to bear his children, who *he* would then control. He'd imagined subjecting her to endless torture. But in the end he'd dismissed them all. For the time being, he was only one mage. The power that he wielded was not sufficient to defeat all the Dirksens who would defend their leader.

Yet the incident with the servant girl had

strengthened his resolve to do *something*. It was clear that Sable was only tolerating him, using him for her own ends. She had no intention of allowing him into the inner circle of influential, powerful Dirksens. He was not a significant figure, he was only a tool.

One thing she hadn't considered, however, was the fact that mages had to be trained. When he'd explained to her that the ability was passed from parent to child, he'd skated over his mother's role in teaching the children. At the time, he'd been downplaying the fact because he'd wanted to make himself appear more impressive, but the omission had worked in his favor in a different way.

Sable Dirksen could breed as many mage offspring as she liked, but they would be useless to her without proper training. Now that he came to think of it, Castiel wasn't sure that he could train anyone else to be a mage even if he'd wanted to. He'd realized long ago that his mother was deliberately a poor teacher. He would do no better than her and probably worse. He also had an inkling that he would lose his talent over time if he didn't practice other things, but he wasn't clear on what they were.

So he had two problems: Sable Dirksen intended on dispensing with him in one way or another eventually, and he needed proper training if he was not to lose his powers. The answer to both of these problems was a single person: Carina. Of all his siblings, she was the only one who had been properly trained. Carina really knew what she was talking about, and she could teach him to be more powerful, so powerful that he could foil Sable's plans to use him for her own ends.

And if he caught Carina, he would have his brothers and sisters too. That would make six mages. With a force as strong as that he wouldn't need Sherrerrs or Dirksens. He could build an empire large and powerful enough to take on and defeat both clans.

That was what he had to do. Finding and capturing his siblings had to be his top priority. Luckily for him, Sable's plans were dovetailing into his own.

The day after he had Enthralled the servant girl and discovered Sable's scheme, Castiel descended the stairs to the great hall in a positive mood. Tiredness stalked him after his long night of worry, but he mentally brushed aside the small discomfort. For the first time since arriving at the mountain castle, he finally felt like he knew exactly where he stood and what he needed to do.

"You seem cheerful this morning," Sable commented as he sat down at the dining table. Kee was also there. Had he spent the previous night with Sable? For once, Castiel experienced no twinge of jealousy. He no longer wanted the small thing that remained for Sable to offer him. He would not sully himself with an intimate relationship with the snake.

"I am cheerful," Castiel replied. "My latest servant is a very pretty, willing young woman. I appreciate you finding her for me after the previous one left so suddenly." He could not resist playing along with Sable's plan in order to see her reaction.

If Commander Kee was aware of Sable's

scheme, he gave no sign of it after hearing Castiel's response. The man ignored him as he always did unless speaking directly to him.

Sable was a master of subterfuge as she, too, didn't do anything other than smile indulgently at his comment. *Bitch!* She wouldn't be smiling for much longer.

***

The day finally came when the fleet was ready, and Castiel and Sable went together to the shuttle that would fly them up to the battlecruiser, *Elsinore*. No one knew what they would encounter at Pirine. Perhaps the population of that world was aware of mages and would rise up to defend them. Perhaps the Dirksens would have a long search on their hands to find Carina and the rest of his siblings. Whatever they might encounter, Sable and Kee had tried to prepare for all eventualities.

All Castiel had to take care of for the trip was his elixir supply. When he'd been aboard the *Nightfall*, his father had brought along a tank of the stuff. Mindful of the fact that he might be involved in a protracted battle, Castiel had made similar preparations. Yet he had insisted on bringing along a supply of ingredients too. The thought of the impending journey had made him painfully aware that without elixir, he was helpless. He didn't even know how to fire a weapon.

Elsinore was a very different ship from *Nightfall*. The passageways were narrower and the bridge held only Kee, as commander of the vessel, the pilot, navigator, and comms and weapons officers. No signs stated the function of each room or section. The crew were expected to know. When Castiel had wandered onto the bridge unwittingly, Kee and the other officers glared at him in silence until he left.

A low-ranking crew member had shown Castiel to his cabin after he disembarked the shuttle. The room was a far cry from the suite his family had been assigned on the *Nightfall*. It was small and contained no private bathroom. He would be forced to use the communal restroom facilities for that section. As if that wasn't bad enough, his bed was one of two, and the crew member who had shown him the place told him not to stow his luggage on the other bunk because someone else would be using it.

Who his bunk mate might be, Castiel had no idea, but whoever it was, it was unconscionable that he had to share at all. But he didn't know what he could do about it. Like it or not, he needed these people for the moment. All he could do was bide his time and plot his revenge for the many insults that had been piled upon him.

Worse still, there wasn't enough space to accommodate the tank of elixir he'd brought along. The container would have to be stowed in the galley, along with ingredients for cooking. It was outrageous. The taste of elixir was disgusting so it was unlikely the liquid would end up in a stew, but nevertheless the fact that it wasn't near to hand made Castiel extremely uncomfortable.

After accidentally walking onto the bridge, Castiel had returned to his room. Or, rather, he tried to return. He had already lost his bearings in the passageways of the large ship. Everywhere seemed to look the same to him, though he guessed there were subtle differences and clues that were unknown to him.

His wanderings resulted in giving him an informal tour of the *Elsinore*. From the mess to the briefing room, he got to know the ship pretty well. He even happened upon Sable's quarters when he spotted her leaving a room. He caught a glimpse of the interior, which was substantially larger and more luxurious than his own.

Castiel had wondered who would be lining up outside the room the next quiet shift, and whether the Dirksen leader would manage to work her way through the entire crew before they reached Pirine.

When he finally found his cabin again, he was irked to see someone lying in the top bunk. He'd left a bag on the bed to claim it, and the person had moved the bag to the bottom bunk.

Castiel was even more irked when the man turned on his side to see who had come in. Reyes Dirksen's hateful visage confronted Castiel. He realized he would be forced to spend weeks cooped up with one of the most loathsome people on Ostillon.

Reyes didn't look surprised to see him. He only smirked and lay down again. So Reyes had been given the information about his bunk mate while Castiel had been kept in the dark. Had Sable Dirksen deliberately put them together to make it easier for Reyes to spy on him?

Castiel sat on the lower bunk, weighing his options. Reyes' move to secure the top bunk was obviously a ploy to signal his dominance. Castiel couldn't allow the step to go unchallenged, but he was unsure of what to do. Hate him as he might, Reyes was older, taller, and stronger than Castiel. He couldn't physically remove him from the bunk.

Also, much as Castiel hated to admit it, Reyes was pretty smart. Castiel doubted he could trick him into giving up the superior sleeping place.

All Castiel had as an advantage was Casting. That was going to be the only thing he could use to force Reyes out of his bed and show him who was boss. Castiel went through a mental list of the Casts he knew: Transport, Locate, Enthrall, Rise, Fire, Heal, Clear, Break, Lock, Repulse, Send and Open were the ones he had practised often. And there was Split too, but he didn't think the Dirksens would take kindly to him using Split on Reyes, satisfying though it might be. They would soon put an end to his affiliation with them through ending his life, mage or not.

No, he needed to do something effective but that didn't cause long-term damage. Castiel made his choice, sipped elixir, and began to Cast.

He opened his eyes and waited for Reyes' response. It wasn't long coming.

"Hey," resounded an angry shout from above. "Put me down!"

Castiel watched with amusement as Reyes floated out from his bunk and across the narrow ceiling. He was twisting and writhing, ineffectively fighting the Cast.

"I said, put me down," Reyes reiterated furiously.

"Are you sure about that?" Castiel asked. He glanced at the floor and back up toward Reyes.

"Looks like a nasty drop to me. But if you insist...."

Reyes, realizing what would happen if Castiel did as he'd asked, said, "Put me back on my bunk, I mean, you moron."

"Those are brave words for someone floating helplessly in my grasp. I'd like an apology."

Reyes only glared at him. Then he cast a look at the floor, as if judging how much he would be hurt by falling the distance. "Go on, drop me. I promise I'll hurt you more than it'll hurt me."

Castiel sat up. He'd had enough of Reyes. He'd had enough of all the Dirksens. If they thought they were going to walk all over him they had another think coming. He would start with Langley Dirksen's son. "Believe me, I can hurt you even more than you can imagine. Did you hear what I did to the Sherrerr admiral? I tore her in two. She died screaming in agony."

He watched Reyes' expression as he registered this fact. He had heard, Castiel could tell. His bravado had begun to weaken.

"And don't think I won't do it," said Castiel. "Just because I can't do it now, it doesn't mean I won't do it at some later date, when I have the power and influence to put a stop to anyone who might want to avenge your life. So you better watch out, Reyes Dirksen. You piss me off, and I won't ever forget it."

Castiel released him, and he hit the floor hard. Reyes yelled in pain and anger, but Castiel's threat had taken effect. Reyes didn't retaliate, and when Castiel climbed up to the top bunk, he didn't respond.

The Dirksen youth sat on the floor for a moment

before getting up and slamming out of the cabin. Castiel looked down and saw blood on the bare metal. He smiled. He must have broken the idiot's nose. Good. He hoped it would serve as a warning to him and to all the other Dirksens. They might treat him like nothing but a tool to be used for the moment, but he would remember it. He would note who showed him favor and who disrespected him, and when the time came they would pay.

CHAPTER NINETEEN

Darius had returned to the tent after another long day spent with the Spirit Mage. Dinner had already been eaten, but Carina had saved some for him. While the others went out to the natural spring at the center of the camp to wash away the dirt and dust accumulated during their day's playing, Carina sat with her sleepy brother, encouraging him to eat more before he went to bed.

Darius did force down a few more mouthfuls before his eyelids drooped and his head nodded. Bryce picked up the little boy and carried him to his sleeping spot at the edge of the large tent.

"He can't go on like this," said Carina after Bryce returned to her side. They sat outside the open tent flap, watching the evening bustle of the camp. Carina wasn't worried about Darius overhearing her. He would be dead to the world until morning, when he would rise and wearily set out for the Spirit Mage's tent again.

"It does seem excessive work for such a young

child," Bryce said. "Have you spoken to Justin or Eira about it?"

"I haven't seen Eira for days. I think she leaves every so often to ferry in new arrivals as a way of avoiding attracting too much attention to the camp. I did speak to Justin, but he only said that learning from the Spirit Mage was Darius' destiny. No other Spirit Mage has appeared in decades, and it's vital that Magda passes on as much knowledge as she can to Darius before she dies. But he's just a little boy."

Carina understood the older mage's perspective: without a Spirit Mage there could be no Matching, and with no Matching the mages and their culture would eventually die out. Yet it seemed wrong to place all that responsibility on the shoulders of a six year old.

"I don't know what to say," said Bryce. "It's mage business."

Carina rubbed her temples. She didn't know what to do for the best. After spending so many years cut off from her mage kindred, Carina felt she knew little more than Bryce did.

"How have the other mages been treating you and Nahla?" she asked him. In her preoccupation with Darius and the novelty of living among hundreds of mages, she'd forgotten that her friend's experience would be very different from her own.

"I'm not sure they know we aren't mages," Bryce replied. "I haven't told anyone, and Nahla has no reason to either. For once, mage reluctance to tell anyone anything is working out for us."

Carina smiled. "But, considering this is a

Matching, have you been approached?" She raised her eyebrows in mock curiosity.

"*Maaaybe,*" Bryce replied. "How about you?"

"Ugh, I have far too much going on to think about things like that. What do you think about spending your life with a mage?"

"I think the ones I know already are enough trouble."

Carina laughed, but then she grew somber. There was one mage who was more than enough trouble for everyone: Castiel. All the mages that, as far as Carina could tell, were 'in charge' knew about her half-brother, but no one had mentioned what should be done about him. Would the responsibility fall to her? And if it did, should she do anything? The more time she spent at the Matching, the more distant the problem of a Dark Mage had become. She didn't think she would need much persuasion to abandon the difficult, dangerous task of putting a stop to his activities.

***

The next day, Carina was walking through the camp and she happened to pass by the Spirit Mage's tent. She was debating whether to go inside and ask to speak to the old woman about Darius, and perhaps about Castiel too when, to her surprise, Magda poked her head through the open flap.

"Carina, please come in for a moment," she said before withdrawing into the tent.

Reluctantly, Carina lifted the flap and went inside. It was the first time she'd seen the interior of Magda's tent. The floor was spread with rugs, and utensils, lamps, and ornaments hung from the struts. Two full bags made of thick, embroidered cloth sat in one corner. The Spirit Mage also had a decorative decanter full of elixir and a couple of beakers.

"Darius isn't here?" Carina asked.

"I sent him home early. The child was tired. Perhaps I have been pushing him too hard."

"Perhaps you have," said Carina, trying but failing to keep an accusatory tone out of her voice.

"You care about him very much, don't you?"

"Of course I do. He's my brother."

"And he's also the only Spirit Mage who has come forward. I know I'm asking a lot of him, Carina, but I have little time left in which to teach him everything I know."

The old woman appeared suddenly frail and ancient, and Carina felt a pang of pity. Yet her sympathies remained with her brother.

"Sit down, dear."

Carina didn't sit. She remained standing, stooped under the tent's low roof. "What do you want to talk to me about?"

Magda, who was cross-legged on the floor, reached up and took Carina's hand in her own. "I feel your presence whenever you walk past my tent. You are full of pain. You are radiating hurt. I think you bear the most suffering of anyone in this camp. I'm surprised Darius can tolerate being around you for long. I want to help you, if I can."

Magda's words surprised Carina. She'd never imagined her presence might bring her brother discomfort. The knowledge hardened her bitterness. "I don't think there's anything you can do to help me, unless you can change the past."

"No one can do that, but sometimes it helps to explore it, accept it, and move on."

"You think I should accept everything that's happened?" Carina remained stubbornly standing. "How's that going to help me?"

"Please, sit. I want to tell you about Faye and Kris."

The mention of her parents' names broke through Carina's defenses. Her resolve not to open herself up to this woman quavered. She lowered herself to her knees. "What do you want to tell me about them?"

"Or perhaps it would be better if I showed your parents to you?"

"Showed them to me? How?" Mages could not keep images or recordings of each other. Everyone knew that.

"Spirit Mages do not only remember stories. One thing I have been teaching your brother is how to memorize what he sees. When he is older and I am dead, he will be able to pass on these images. It's the only way we have of keeping a record of our kind. Carina, I was at the Matching where your parents met. I remember them. Would you like to see them?"

Was there anything in the galaxy Carina wanted more than to see her parents again? Perhaps, but not many things. She would give a lot to see them as they had been when they were young and before harm had come to them. "Yes, I would."

"Good. Close your eyes. I will Send my memories to you. It may take some time, so please have patience."

Carina did as the woman asked. Outside, the

carefree sounds of the camp continued. Carina could hear people talking and laughing. In the distance, musical instruments played and people sang along. Someone had started a fire and Carina could hear it crackling. Faint smells of food cooking invaded the tent.

But Carina saw only darkness, until she saw them. The setting was the same. She could see the camp and the people, almost identical to the present, but the scene must have been from more than twenty years previously.

Ma and Ba were walking through the long grass at the edge of the camp, just talking, but the look of love that passed between them was so strong it was almost palpable. Ma looked almost exactly how Carina remembered her as a child, but more distinct and real. Her face was fresh and plump, not thin and sallow as it had been after years of torture from Stefan Sherrerr. Ba was a young, strong man, maybe not as handsome or strong-looking as some, but his expression was honest and kind.

It was too much. Instead of bringing her joy, the sight opened deep wounds inside Carina—wounds that had festered under scars she had forced herself to grow. The image of her parents so young and innocent, so full of love and happiness, so unaware of the horrors that lay in their future, caused Carina almost unbearable agony.

Her eyes snapped open. "Stop! Stop it!" She leapt up, knocking her head against a hanging cooking pot, and ran out of the tent. Momentarily blinded by the strong sunlight and confused by her emotional state, Carina paused. Then she set off through the camp, hardly knowing where she was going.

What had Magda been thinking? She was either an idiot or a sadist. Carina couldn't understand why the old woman would subject her to something so painful. She had made everything worse, not better.

Carina strode on, unheeding of the glances of the young mages, until she found she had somehow made her way back to her own tent.

She stumbled inside. The place was dark and quiet. Only Bryce was there, stretched out and snoozing. Carina's entrance woke him.

"Hey," he said, "what's—"

"Where's Darius? Magda said she sent him back because he looked tired."

"He's gone to play in the prairie," Bryce replied. "I guess he missed his brothers and sisters more than sleep."

When she realized Bryce was alone in the tent and the children were not around, Carina turned and fastened the entrance.

"What are you doing?"

Carina had gone over to Bryce. He sat up. Welcoming the news they would be alone for a while, she kissed him hard on the mouth. For a moment Bryce was too shocked to respond, but then he kissed her back and pulled her close to his chest.

Carina remembered the first night they'd met, on Ithiya. Bryce had kissed her then. She hadn't forgotten what a good kisser he was. As they held each other tightly, her pain began to lose its edge. She needed to push it all away, push the hurt back down where it belonged.

But then Bryce stopped kissing her. He looked into her surprised eyes, and disengaged himself from their embrace. He gripped her arms, holding her distant from him. "Carina, what is this? What's going on?"

"What? Nothing's going on. Let's do it." Carina leaned in to kiss him again, but Bryce moved his head backward.

He gave her a strange look. "Has something happened? Something's wrong, isn't it? This isn't like you."

Carina could feel her cheeks turning scarlet. "I don't know what you're talking about." She tried to kiss him again but he turned away.

"Carina, I—"

"For stars' sake! Do I have to put in a request?"

Bryce was shaking his head. "Something's rattled you. I can tell. Is this what you used to do with your merc buddies to get over your feelings when you were upset?" His tone was challenging.

Carina moved away from him, blinking away tears, shame tingling every fiber of her being. "How dare you…. If you don't want me, that's fine. Only I got a different impression."

"I'm sorry. That didn't come out how I meant it."

But Carina was already leaving. She couldn't bear the embarrassment. How would she look Bryce in the eye now?

"Carina, please don't go. It's just that it wouldn't be right for our first time, not like this. Not because you're hurting. I don't want it to be—"

But she didn't hear any more. Carina was outside the tent and walking away. She left the camp by the quickest route and marched onto the prairie. She continued walking, long miles, into the evening and the night.

Carina didn't return until the pale gray pre-dawn light suffused the sky. The camp was quiet and everyone was asleep.

CHAPTER TWENTY

Castiel hated traveling aboard a starship. He hated the claustrophobic conditions and the inconvenience. He also hated all his traveling companions: Commander Kee and his crew, the troops on board, Sable Dirksen, another clan member called Barrett, and most of all Reyes. Castiel figured that Sable had made them bunk mates so that Reyes could spy on him. Though he'd put Reyes in his place by ousting him from the top bunk, Castiel was at a loss about what else to do against the smug upstart.

Castiel's position remained uncertain and shaky. Sable could use him, but he was not indispensable. To improve his position, he needed people he could directly control. Until then, he didn't want to risk the disfavor of the Dirksens. Providing he did their bidding they would tolerate him as an ally, perhaps. As soon as he stepped out of line his days would be numbered.

Since the incident when Castiel had dropped

Reyes on his face, the two roommates hadn't spoken a word to each other, which was exactly how Castiel liked it. However, it was clear that Reyes was well liked by everyone aboard the vessel. He had plenty of social interactions, while no one spoke a word more than was necessary to Castiel.

Mealtimes were the worst. Sable sat with Kee, Barrett, Reyes, and a couple of high-ranking officers. Castiel was not invited to sit at the same table, and Sable had given him an icy stare the first time he'd approached the group. When he sat at the tables for the rest of the crew, no one sat with him.

As the weeks had worn on, his anger at this unsubtle ostracization had grown.

The final straw came when Castiel returned to his cabin at the beginning of the quiet shift to find that Reyes had once more occupied the top bunk.

Castiel could hardly believe the older boy's audacity and stupidity. Didn't he know he was about to end up face down on the floor again, only thrown, not dropped this time?

"What the hell do you think you're doing?" Castiel exclaimed. "Get down from there. That's my bed and you know it."

Reyes leaned over the edge of the bunk and glared at Castiel. "Make me."

"All right, I will. You asked for it."

Castiel took out his elixir bottle. He wondered how hard he could throw Reyes without any retribution from Sable. Then fury seized him. He was sick and tired of everyone's treatment of him. He would throw Reyes from the ceiling to the floor and perhaps bounce him around the cabin with some Transport Casts. Maybe he would stop short of actually killing him.

He didn't care what Sable said or did. He had enough elixir to inflict some serious damage on someone before anyone could stop him, come what may.

Reyes was watching him. Castiel took a swig from his canister without breaking eye contact with the Dirksen brat. When the liquid hit his tongue, he spat it out in surprise. The taste was wrong. It wasn't elixir. He took another sip. The liquid was plain water. Castiel stared at the canister. How had they managed to switch the contents? He kept it by his side all the time.

Reyes was laughing. "I wish you could see your face. It's quite the picture." His laugh faded and his expression grew malevolent. "Not so cocky now, huh?"

Fear began to creep up on Castiel. Without his elixir, he felt naked and very vulnerable. He turned to leave the cabin, but there came the sound of movement behind him. A heavy weight landed on his back. Reyes had jumped onto him. Castiel's face hit the door. He heard the crunch of his nose breaking. Agony stabbed at him and hot blood gushed out.

Castiel yelled. Reyes' impact had forced him to the floor. Two hands grabbed his hair and lifted his head before slamming it into the floor, again and again. Reyes was yelling at him.

"You're nothing but a traitor, Castiel Sherrerr, betraying your own kind. Your sister isn't even a Sherrerr but she refused to help us. *She* had some honor. You're nothing but a slime ball. A turd. A faithless, disloyal, two-faced toad."

Finally, the banging of Castiel's head on the floor stopped. Reyes climbed off his back. Castiel heard him stand, then Reyes' boot thudded into Castiel's side and pain erupted again. Reyes kicked him three or four more times. He moved away and the door opened.

"You'll be given your potion when *we* want you to use it," said Reyes. "And if you use it on one of us again, we'll kill you."

The door closed.

Castiel lay still. The blood from his nose had formed a lukewarm, sticky pool around his face. He had never hurt so much in his life. His head throbbed. It felt like Reyes was still banging it on the floor. His side ached where Reyes' boot had landed. Castiel fought the urge to vomit. He fought the urge to cry even more. He would not shed tears like a baby. He was a man, and he would behave like one. That was what Father would have wanted.

In time, Castiel found the strength to sit up, though he didn't move from the floor. He sat in his blood and brooded on his pain and hurt. He would never forget this moment. He had tried to help the Dirksens. All he'd desired had been to progress to his rightful place at the head of the clan. If they'd allowed him that, they all could have benefited. But instead the clan had chosen to use him, like he was nothing. They wanted what he had to offer, but they refused to give anything back, not even the recognition he was owed.

So be it. Castiel had played along and so he

would continue, for exactly as long as it suited him. Then they would all pay, and pay dearly.

***

As if Reyes' attack had been a trigger, Castiel noticed a deepening in the coldness he experienced from everyone aboard the ship. He was not confined to his cabin, as he'd suspected might happen, but no one spoke a word to him. No one looked at him. If he didn't move aside in the passageways, the crew would walk right into him. It was like he was invisible, a ghost who didn't know he was dead yet.

The supply of elixir he'd brought aboard the ship had, predictably, disappeared from the galley. When he asked the cook where it was, the man had looked through him as though he wasn't there. He guessed the liquid would reappear when they arrived at Pirine, but he wasn't even sure of that.

As he drifted about the ship while the seemingly endless journey dragged on, Castiel wondered why, if he was no longer considered an ally but only someone to be used, the Dirksens hadn't put him in the brig. When the answer to this puzzle hit him, his cheeks turned fiery red with anger and shame. The reason the Dirksens hadn't locked him up wasn't due to fear of retribution, but the exact opposite: they didn't fear him at all. They hadn't confined him because they couldn't be bothered.

This new understanding hit hard, and it was as much as Castiel could do to not take a mess knife and murder Sable Dirksen. The attention she'd shown him, scant as it was, had all been a sham. She'd only been playing with him, drawing as much information from him as she could. Now that she had what she wanted, all pretense was gone.

Fanciful ideas of revenge Castiel had formed previously devolved into a simmering black hatred, not only of the Dirksens, but of everyone else who had disrespected him over the years. He hated all of humanity, in fact. The only person who had ever treated him as he deserved was Father, and he was dead.

Castiel decided he would never show mercy to any human being.

Then the announcement came. The *Elsinore* had arrived at Pirine.

CHAPTER TWENTY-ONE

Carina's experience of the Matching had turned from pleasure to bitter unhappiness. Her friendship with Bryce was ruined, Parthenia still hated her, and the Spirit Mage seemed intent on overwhelming Darius with knowledge.

The old woman seemed to cause her nothing but heartache. Though Darius' admiration and almost hero-worship of her had been over the top and unwarranted, Carina had been touched by it. The news that her presence caused her beloved brother pain had come as a shock, and she didn't know how to deal with it.

The only saving graces of her family's current situation were that Oriana and Ferne were finally, truly happy, and that Nahla was coming out of her shell. Her little personality was blossoming and it warmed Carina's heart to see it. The girl had spent so long in Castiel's shadow and following around at his heels, Carina had feared she would never get over it. But the kindness of Oriana and Ferne along with the young mages at the camp had paid off.

Nahla no longer spoke in whispers or hung back from joining in activities.

If only Carina could similarly blossom. Though she was younger than many of the women and men at the Matching, she felt older and battle-worn, and she didn't know if she would ever be fixed.

Various young men had approached her over the weeks in subtle but unmistakable ways. Carina had equally subtly rejected their advances. She was in no mood for love, and she had alienated the one person she might have considered in that way, through her clumsy proposition.

What was it Bryce had asked her during that shameful moment? Something about resorting to doing that with her fellow mercs when something upset her. She hadn't thought about it, but maybe he had a point.

Having nothing better to do one evening, Carina decided to listen to another of the Spirit Mage's stories. Darius and Nahla were already asleep and Oriana and Ferne agreed to remain in the tent to look after them. Carina walked through the camp in the heavy twilight toward the large, central fire where the Spirit Mage told her stories.

The Spirit Mage was sitting on the far side of the fire so Carina couldn't see her. She could only hear the old woman's story, which had already begun. Carina sat cross-legged. She rested an elbow on one knee and her chin on her palm, closed her eyes, and began to listen.

> *The Dark Mage had been working in secret—*

Carina's ears pricked up. This was the first story of a Dark Mage the Spirit Mage had told as far as

Carina knew. She listened more intently, hoping to hear something useful.

When the story was over, despite the late hour, Carina decided to speak to the Spirit Mage before she returned to her tent. She had, if she was honest, all but given up on the idea of returning to Ostillon to try to find her mage half-brother and prevent him from exercising his powers for evil. But the Spirit Mage's story had forced her to reconsider. Perhaps mages did have a duty to protect the rest of humankind from the evil possibilities of Casting.

Carina caught up to the old woman. "I'd like to talk about what you said tonight, if you don't mind."

"I don't mind at all. Did you enjoy the story?"

"I don't know if 'enjoy' is the right word to describe how I felt about it. Did you hear that I have a half-brother who is a Dark Mage?"

"I did. The mage council has decided to wait to see what eventuates before making a decision about what we should do."

"The mage council?"

"Ah," said Magda, putting her hand to her mouth. "I shouldn't have let that slip. I apologize. I'm getting old. Please don't ask me any more about what I said."

It wasn't hard to guess the facts behind the old woman's slip up. Justin, Jace, the *Haihu's* captain, and other, older mages Carina had seen were clearly members of some organization involved in overseeing the activities of mages. Like most things in mage life, the council was secret.

But one thing was clear: the mage council was

not going to tackle Castiel, or at least not until he did something truly dreadful. If anyone was going to take away his ability to commit evil acts, it was down to his family.

"I'm sorry that showing you the images of your parents upset you the other day," the old woman continued. "That wasn't my intention."

"It's okay," Carina replied. "I understand now that you were trying to help. You couldn't have known the effect it would have. I didn't know it myself. And though it did make me unhappy at the time, I'm glad I have those memories now."

The Spirit Mage reached out to Carina's forearm and gripped it tightly. "I try to help, you see, but I don't always succeed. I was only given the gift of feeling what others feel, but not the wisdom of how to make them feel better. It's been the labor of my life to learn that, but I was a poor student."

Though Carina was no Spirit Mage, she sensed the woman's deep sorrow and for the first time saw things from her perspective. The woman had an unenviable responsibility. She carried thousands of years of mage lore in her mind and it was her duty to pass that on as fully and faithfully as she could. If she failed it would mean the loss of their history and everything that made them who they were. Carina had only been seeing her as someone who was taking Darius away and overloading his young mind. She had seen the toll it was taking on him. He was constantly fatigued and low spirited.

But the Spirit Mage was trying to save their clan before it was too late, and Darius was her only means of doing so.

"And I'm glad you don't hate me for what I did," said the mage. "Though I don't think that after this Matching we will part as friends."

"Huh? Why not?" Carina had a sudden sense of foreboding.

"Please come inside so we can talk."

They were at the old woman's tent. She lifted the flap to invite Carina to enter first and then followed her. The interior was dark, only the light from the dying campfire creating a glow through the wall. The woman lit a lamp and invited Carina to sit down.

As she had done when she'd shown Carina her memory of her parents, the Spirit Mage sat opposite her and took Carina's hands in her own.

"I wish you were older, and one of Darius' parents. But you are the closest person he has to a parent now. Carina, there's no easy way to say this. I know how much Darius means to you."

Carina's stomach tightened. What was the woman going to say?

"When the Matching is over, Darius must come with me."

Carina snatched her hands away. "No way. Absolutely not. He's far too young. He needs to be with the family he has left. He needs to be with me."

The Spirit Mage's eyes were sad. "I guessed that would be how you would feel. Nevertheless…."

"Nevertheless nothing! You're right. I am the closest thing Darius has to a parent. I have the final say over what he does and where he goes. And I don't give permission for you to take him anywhere. He's six years old, for stars' sake. He's much too young to leave his family." Despite her words, Carina was deeply conflicted. Keeping Darius by her side meant he would be subjected to her emotional pain.

"He is very young," said the mage. "But he will be well cared for. Carina, please listen to me. This is unavoidable. Jace, Justin, and all the others agree. The work I've done with Darius so far is only the beginning of what I must teach him. If I were only to see him at Matchings, it would take decades to impart everything he must learn. And I have so little time left. He has to live with me so he can study every day. The future of our kind depends on it."

"I don't care," Carina retorted. "He's just a little boy. It's too much to ask of him. It isn't fair."

"I agree. It isn't fair. And yet that's the situation we find ourselves in. Such is the lot of mages. We sacrifice so much in order to keep our heritage continuing."

"Then maybe it's time to give up."

The Spirit Mage had been looking downward, but at this she raised her head. "You mean give up being mages?"

"Maybe we should. Maybe it's the only sensible thing to do. Ma told me once that it was only because someone once stumbled on the secret of our abilities millenia ago that we realized we weren't the same as other people. If we give up, we'll go back to being like everyone else. No running, no hiding, no persecution, torture, and rape. Did you hear what my mother went through?"

"No, I didn't, but I know. It's written on your heart."

Carina's eyes stung. "And my father—murdered. All because they wanted to use their powers to help people. Now you're telling me you have to rip a little boy away from the people who love him so he can help to keep magehood alive. Why? What's the point? We don't use our abilities to improve humankind, we only use them to help ourselves, in secret. We live our lives in fear. Maybe it's time to call it a day, right now."

She stood up, crouching under the low ceiling. "You're right. I am the person who is responsible for Darius, and I say no. He isn't going anywhere with you. He's coming with us. In fact, I don't even know why we're here. I'm not interested in Matching with anyone and all my brothers and sisters are too young. We'll be leaving in the morning."

Carina left the tent without looking back. She was furious. How dare the old witch think she could just take Darius away for her own ends? He wasn't a sack of flour to be carted around, passed to whoever wanted him.

When she arrived at her tent, everyone was asleep. In the dim light, Carina surveyed the low, black humps that represented everyone she cared about. No one was going to take any of them away from her, and she would kill anyone who tried. She had already lost three of the most important people in her life and endured years of isolation and loneliness. She wasn't going to lose anyone else.

Carina tiptoed between the sleeping forms to

reach her spot and slipped under her blanket. She was settling down, her mind still whirling from the conversation with the Spirit Mage, when she felt someone gently grasp her foot. It was Bryce, who slept along from her.

"Everything okay?" he whispered.

Carina was too choked up to answer. She silently shook her head, though she doubted Bryce could see the gesture. A moment later she heard him leave his spot and crawl over to her. He lay down opposite her. She couldn't see much more of him than the glint of his eyes in the darkness.

His proximity brought back the vivid memory of her failed seduction and her face became hot. She was glad he couldn't see her.

"What's up?" he murmured.

"The mages want Darius to leave us and go with the Spirit Mage when the Matching is over."

"You're kidding!"

"I wish I was."

"You aren't going to let them take him, right?"

"Of course not. But that means we have to leave tomorrow, early."

"Okay, that's what we'll do. I'm not sure how far the closest city is, but we can make it there."

"What if they try to stop us?" Carina asked. She didn't know how the mage council would react, and, stupidly, in her anger she'd announced her intention. There would be no slipping away quietly while no one was looking. She didn't relish the idea of trying to fight off a thousand mages in order to leave, even with Darius' exceptional ability on their side.

"I don't think they will," Bryce replied. "They'll

probably only try to argue you out of it, but I doubt they'll try to stop you physically. Mages seem to be gentle, non-confrontational people."

"I wouldn't be too sure about that. I wouldn't have survived long as a merc by being gentle and non-confrontational."

"Good point."

A pause stretched out.

"Bryce…I'm sorry—"

He kissed her. "It's okay."

***

The following day, the news that they were going to leave the Matching didn't go down well among Carina's brothers and sisters, with one exception.

After Carina made the announcement, Parthenia said, "So we're finally going back to Ostillon to deal with Castiel?"

"I think so," said Carina. Maybe she'd been wrong all along. If the Matching had taught her anything, it was that her family should stick together and take care of their own, whether that meant a small boy's welfare or preventing his elder brother from committing terrible acts.

"Great! At last."

"But don't I have to stay with the Spirit Mage?" asked Darius.

"No, not any longer," Carina replied. "You've spent enough time with her already." As she spoke knots of anxiety formed in her stomach. Was she doing the right thing? She just didn't know. Nothing seemed right, but if one thing was for sure, her family was not going to be split up again.

Oriana and Ferne looked glum but didn't say anything. Nahla began to pack their few belongings.

"How are we going to leave?" Darius asked.

It was a good point. They had arrived via the *Haihu's* shuttle. Even if the mages agreed to their leaving, Carina doubted they would give them a ride to the nearest spaceport. She didn't know how the other people at the camp had traveled there, or where the nearest city was. Perhaps leaving the Matching wouldn't be so easy after all.

The tent flap was open, and the morning sunlight was suddenly cut off as a large figure appeared in the entrance. It was Jace.

The children stopped their packing, but the newcomer's expression registered that he understood what was happening. "The Spirit Mage Sent to me when I woke up. She told me you might be leaving. I see that you are."

His tone was neutral. Carina couldn't guess what he thought of her decision or if he would try to stop them. She sized him up. Though he was far larger than her, she might be able to take him if he didn't know how to fight.

"That's right," she replied. "I'm not prepared to let Darius go with the Spirit Mage."

"I understand...Is it okay if I come in so we can talk?"

"I guess so," Carina said warily. "But I'm warning you, if you try to stop us you'll regret it."

Jace halted as he entered the tent, stooping low, and looked Carina in the eyes. "It seems you haven't learned much about mages in your time here." He sat down and continued, "Have you considered that you could also live on the Spirit Mage's world and see Darius whenever you wanted to?"

"I-I..." Carina felt suddenly foolish. "No, I hadn't considered that. But he's too young to be trained in this way. The fate of all mages is too heavy a burden to place on the shoulders of a young child. Besides, we have other work to do. We must find our Dark Mage brother and stop him from hurting anyone."

"So, you don't want Darius to live with an old lady in safety on a backwater planet, but you're happy to take him into conflict with a Dark Mage?"

The way Jace put it made Carina think again, but she quickly came to the same decision. "I know how it sounds, but I will keep Darius safe, and the rest of the younger children too. You have to understand that we're a family. We have our own path to follow. And though you say the Spirit Mage lives on a safe, backwater planet, that's exactly what Ostillon was before the Dirksens decided to make it their base. The same with my home planet—safe, boring, and dirt poor. But that didn't stop Regians from paying us a visit and starting a massacre. Nowhere in this galactic sector is safe with a Dark Mage running loose. Castiel is our brother and it's up to us to neutralize him. Then we can leave the Sherrerrs and the Dirksens to continue their feud while we search for Earth."

Carina took a breath. There, she'd said it, crazy as it sounded.

Jace's eyebrows rose. "You have it all figured out, don't you?" His words sounded mocking but his intonation was serious. "If that's your wish, no one here will stop you."

"You won't?" asked Carina. She found it hard to

believe he would give in so easily. "But the Spirit Mage was telling me it's vital that Darius is trained by her. She seemed to think the future of mage lore depended on it."

"She may well be correct. On the other hand, perhaps another Spirit Mage will appear. Maybe someone older than Darius, who has been lost or delayed. Who knows what may happen? But I am convinced your intention is sincere and you are capable of protecting those in your charge. It is clear you would give your life before you allowed them to come to harm. In any case, you have always been free to leave whenever you wanted. It would go against everything we stand for to keep you here by force."

Relief washed over Carina. She wouldn't have to fight Jace. He was a good man and she would have regretted it.

"Do you have a plan for reaching the city?" he asked.

"Not exactly. I thought we would have to walk there."

"You aren't well equipped for that. I will wait outside while you finish packing, then I'll take you to your transportation."

It didn't take them long to pack. They had the clothes they'd been wearing when they'd arrived, plus a few donated belongings. Nahla had been given a doll made from dried grass that she treated as the most precious thing she'd ever owned. Her attachment to the toy was odd considering all the valuable things that she must have been given in her former life.

When they were ready, they stepped out into the

sunlight. A pile of full, cloth bags had appeared beside their tent.

"Who do they belong to?" asked Oriana.

"They're all of yours," Jace replied. "Word has gotten around that you're leaving. People know you have nothing so they wanted to help you out."

Carina's throat felt thick and her eyes stung. "Even though we're taking away the next Spirit Mage?"

"Even so," said Jace.

Carina's surprise and gratitude almost made her change her mind about leaving. But she was convinced she was doing the right thing. She spotted the edges of weapon butts poking out of a bulky bag. "Are those guns?"

"The city isn't well policed," replied Jace. "Those are for your protection, but I wouldn't go flashing them around if I were you. There's no sense in inviting trouble."

"I understand," said Carina. "Please give everyone our thanks."

"I will, but they don't need it. They're only doing the same for you as they would for any fellow mage. That's one reason we have survived for so long, I believe. We always help each other. Are you ready?"

"Yes. Let's go." Carina told the others to take a bag and picked up the weapons bag herself. The heavy weight of steel was comforting and familiar. She felt a whole lot safer when armed.

"Oh, we have lots of elixir," said Darius, opening a bag.

"Good," said Carina. "Come on, everyone. The morning's passing and we have a long journey ahead of us."

Jace led them through the camp, past the central fire pit, now black and faintly smoking, and into a section where Carina had never been. The young mages were rising, preparing their breakfasts, and talking. The scene was one Carina had seen many times but now she realized she might be seeing it for the last time, a pang of sadness hit her. Would she ever see her people gathered in such numbers again? She doubted it. A mage's life was a lonely one. All the more reason to keep her family close together.

"Do you think you'll ever be back?" asked Bryce, as if he'd read her thoughts.

"I don't think so."

"But what if you're Summoned again?"

"Oh, I wouldn't go. What would be the point?"

And with those words, Carina realized that at some point over the previous few days, she had found herself already Matched. Bryce held her gaze for a moment as they came to their mutual understanding, and then he nodded, satisfied.

At the edge of the campsite stood Justin, Eira, the *Haihu's* captain, and the ship's hands, Ren and Ione.

"Are we taking the shuttle?" Carina asked.

"No," replied Jace. "My brother and the ship's crew are here to help Transport you all. We'll go to a location a few kilometers from the city and then you can make your way in quietly. We try to attract as little attention as possible."

"We? You're coming too?"

"Of course. I will stay with you until I'm sure you're safe."

"Thank you."

"It's no problem. Are you all ready?" Jace asked Carina's siblings.

As soon as it was clear they were all prepared to depart the camp, Justin and the other mages Transported them.

***

If it weren't for the city she could see in the distance, Carina would have thought she hadn't moved. They were surrounded by the high, tough grass of the prairie. Except she could hear something else.

"Oh no," Parthenia blurted. "It's those horrible animals."

Carina turned to see what her sister was talking about. Several meters away thirty or forty large, four-legged animals were enclosed by a fence. A dwelling stood next to the fence along with a barn. The door opened and a middle-aged woman came out.

"Are you talking about my horses, young lady?" asked the woman. "They aren't horrible."

Parthenia flushed and looked at her feet.

"You better get used to them," said Jace, smiling. "They're your transportation."

"Huh?" Carina asked. "How can they take us into the city?"

"We have to sit on their backs," said Ferne. "There were horses on Ostillon too. Didn't you ever see any? The first night we spent there, we slept in a barn that held horses. I think they're nice."

"Do we have to use them?" asked Parthenia.

Jace replied, "There are no roads hereabouts. That's what helps to keep this place unnoticed. It's the safest route into the city for all of you. We can't risk people popping up out of nowhere all the time."

Carina sized up the creatures. She could see how it might be possible to sit on their backs, though it didn't look like it would be very comfortable.

"So, will the little ones sit with the grown ups?" the woman asked Jace.

"Yes, that would be best."

"Okay, can you give me a hand to saddle them up?"

Jace left them to help the woman.

"I'm not sure about this," said Parthenia.

She addressed her comment to Carina. It was the first time she'd spoken normally to her sister since Carina had Enthralled her.

"It'll be all right," Carina replied. "I'm sure Jace wouldn't have brought us here otherwise."

They stood and watched the woman catch and then attach some kind of harness to the animals and then put a seat on their backs.

As she led the first horse over, the woman said, "You don't have anything to be frightened of. I picked the quietest, gentlest ones. They're a bit slow, but they won't bolt or try to throw you off. This is Rainbow. Who wants her?"

"I do," said Oriana. Her face was bright with excitement.

"Step up here then," the woman said, gesturing to a box next to the fence.

When Oriana was in place, the woman led the horse over to her and explained how to climb onto it. Soon, Oriana was sitting on the back of the beast looking like she'd just received the best birthday present she'd ever had. The woman taught her how to hold the straps that controlled the creature's head and told it which way to go. She also told her how gentle kicks would encourage it to go faster.

"But you'll only be walking into town," the woman concluded. "The horses will follow Jace's naturally. You won't need to do much."

While Carina had been watching Oriana, Jace had mounted one of the horses and walked it over.

"Jump up onto the step, Darius," he said. "You can ride in front of me."

A shadow of distrust passed over Carina's heart. Was Jace about to disappear with the precious new Spirit Mage? She caught Jace watching her expression. He gave a slight shake of his head as if rankled.

Darius leapt onto the steps and allowed Jace to lift him onto the horse. He was beaming with pleasure the same as Oriana.

Soon, they were all seated aboard the animals, their provisions slung over their shoulders. Jace thanked the woman and said goodbye. Carina noticed that he hadn't once spoken her name. He kicked his horse and rode to the front, heading out along a track worn through the grass. Carina's animal didn't need any direction from her. It followed Jace's without Carina's guidance or urging.

Parthenia looked scared and was holding on tightly, but Carina guessed she would be fine in time. The motion of the horse as it walked was soothing.

"Do horses live on many planets in this region?" Ferne asked Jace.

"Only five planets as far as I'm aware," the older mage replied. "I've heard that mages brought them on their colony ship when leaving Earth."

"I can't imagine these creatures living on a starship," said Carina.

"Perhaps they brought them in deep sleep," Jace replied.

Deep sleep was used to travel long distances that took months or years, such as when traveling out of the galactic sector. Carina had never been on a ship that had that kind of equipment.

"Do you think that's how the mages first came to this region?" she asked Jace.

"It's certainly possible. Sadly, we'll never know. That first ship must have rotted to dust thousands of years ago."

Carina got the sudden urge to talk more with the man. He would soon be leaving them and she might never see him again. She guessed he probably knew more than most mages about their origins and that first journey.

She gave her horse an experimental kick. The animal responded by moving a little faster. By trial and error, Carina finally found herself riding next to Jace. He glanced across at her with a quizzical but not displeased look.

"Is it correct that mages were the first colonists of Ostillon?" she asked.

"That's generally thought to be the case, but how did you know?"

Carina told him about the religious scripture she'd read on the planet, which seemed to tell the story from the viewpoint of the second wave of colonists, who were regular humans.

"Hmm.... Mage lore relates that story a little differently, but that seems to be basically what happened. The mages tried to get along with the newcomers, but the new arrivals were too frightened of mage powers. It was the same story as what happened on Earth: the mages were persecuted and driven into hiding. There's actually a place in the mountains not far from the capital that was their final refuge until it was decided that the best course of action would be to split up and scatter to the stars to live in secret and only meet at certain gatherings like the Matching."

"You mean there are other gatherings?" asked Carina.

"You know I can't tell you any more, Carina."

"Okay, I understand. Sorry for asking. But...."

Jace rolled his eyes.

"Do you know the Ostillonians burn Characters as a ritual?"

"I do. They also burn the Map."

"Ah, of course." Carina recalled the moment in the temple when she'd seen a paper thrown into the ritual flames. "The paper covered in dots."

"That's right. It's the Map, and it has numbers too."

Carina sat upright in her saddle and swiveled to face the older mage. "You're kidding! They must be coordinates."

"If they are, they're wrong."

"How do you know?"

"Because people have traveled to them. They lead to empty space."

"What people?"

"Mages who lived a long time before you or I. You aren't the first person to try to find their way back, you know. Earth is lost, Carina. You should forget about it."

"Do you think the entire system was blown apart?"

"I think they would have found the remains of it at those coordinates if that were the case, but according to the stories there was nothing. Either Earth never existed and our origin story is a myth, or the coordinates are wrong."

The conversation was such a revelation, Carina rode on in silence for a while as she digested the information. "I think the coordinates must be wrong. They were written so long ago, we no longer use the same system for mapping the galaxy."

"Whatever the answer is, it means we can never go back. It would be impossible to find an unknown planet without correct coordinates. The galaxy is too vast to search."

"But we know they came to Ostillon or a nearby planet first. That's a start."

"We know nothing of the kind. It's all guesses. And, anyway, if you did manage to find Earth, what are you imagining you'll find there? Mages left the place for a reason. What makes you think it's livable or we'll be welcomed back?"

Carina didn't have a good answer to the questions. "I guess I would just like to see where my ancestors came from. And maybe I hope that things might have changed there in the intervening time. Wouldn't it be wonderful if we had a home where we could live without fear of torture and slavery?"

"Mages had that on Ostillon, and look what happened. It's the nature of humans to fear anyone different from themselves and to persecute them. Human nature will never change."

"I used to think that too, but Bryce taught me differently."

Jace's expression twisted as if he were uncomfortable. "There's an exception to every rule."

As they rode, the city drew nearer, and soon they reached the end of a street of cheap, one-story houses and shacks that petered out into the prairie.

"This is where we part ways," Jace announced. He halted his horse and immediately the rest of the animals followed suit, except for Oriana's, which turned its head as if wanting to go home.

"Whoa, there," Jace called at the animal, causing it to stop and shuffle restlessly on the dirt track. "Don't try to get down yourselves," he said to the younger riders. "Wait for me to help you."

Carina watched him dismount and then did the same herself as he lifted Darius down. Soon, everyone was off their horses and waiting while Jace tied a line between the animals to lead them home.

When he was finally done, he strode to Carina and enveloped her in an unexpected hug. Though she wasn't a small woman, she felt crushed in the large man's embrace. He released her and thrust a packet into her hands. "It's the local currency," he explained. "Earned by honest means."

"But I can't accept—"

"We're mages. We help each other. One day you'll have the opportunity to help someone else. Now, that money should pay for a few night's lodging and food. Simple, low-paid work shouldn't be too hard to find. Good luck, Carina, and the rest of you. I hope our paths cross again someday."

Before Carina had the opportunity to answer, Jace had swung himself up onto his large horse and walked it away. They watched as the train of animals slowly departed.

"It looks like that's it," said Carina. "Let's find somewhere to stay."

CHAPTER TWENTY-TWO

Kee was taking a landing party to Pirine's largest city, Ulcawell. Castiel was to accompany the group and, worse still, Reyes was to be his 'minder'. He was enjoying brandishing a weapon.

Kee addressed the team in the *Elsinore's* shuttle bay. He had assembled eight soldiers and four regular crew as well as Castiel and Reyes. Barrett Dirksen was also coming along. Castiel had not figured out the man's role in the Dirksen clan. Slim, dark-skinned, and black-haired, he dressed plainly but expensively, as Sable did, though Castiel could not see an actual family resemblance. But his status was clear from Kee's deference to him.

"There's no point in trying to hide who we are," said Kee to the party. "A battlecruiser in orbit is kind of hard to disguise, and as soon as we arrive at Ulcawell spaceport we'll be met with plenty of questions. But I'm sure I don't need to remind you that you are not to give away the true reason for our presence on Pirine. If anyone asks what we're doing here, the answer you must give is that we're paying a diplomatic visit as a gesture of friendship from the Dirksen Federation."

So that's Barrett Dirksen's role, thought Castiel. The man was to play the diplomat while Kee got on with the real task of locating Carina and Castiel's other brothers and sisters.

"Remember," Kee continued, "your role is to mingle with the local population. Ask about new arrivals in Pirine. A group of five children and a young woman looking after them. This is a quiet place with a small population. Someone might have noticed them. Also ask about reports of odd happenings, things that cannot ordinarily happen."

"Permission to speak, sir," said a soldier.

"Yes, corporal?"

"Could you give us a few examples?"

Kee turned to Castiel. "What do you suggest?"

Castiel was about to refuse to answer, but Reyes was one step ahead of him. He knocked the butt of a weapon into Castiel's shoulder and said, "Tell him."

A quiet fury had been simmering in Castiel for days, threatening to boil over, but he managed to keep a lid on it. "You might hear reports of people acting strangely, as if not under their own control, doors unlocking themselves, things moved by unseen hands. That kind of thing. Mages can also Transport themselves from place to place, so you might hear of people suddenly disappearing or appearing. But we're usually very careful never to do that anywhere that it might be noticed."

Except when trying to escape. The moment he

was allowed to get his hands on some elixir, that was Castiel's plan. He would Cast Transport and put as much distance between himself and Kee, Reyes, and the rest of the landing party as he could. Pirine might be the middle of nowhere in terms of significance in the galactic sector, but he would rather be stranded there than spend another minute under the control of the Dirksens.

His experience of the last few days had taught him that all his plans had come to nothing. He had become a slave to the clan, to be treated the same as His father had treated his mother and his mage siblings.

Yet he had not resigned himself to a sense of inevitability about his fate. Castiel had only given up on relying on others to assign him the power that was fitting to his abilities. Now he knew that if he was to rise to prominence he would have to do it alone.

Only first he had to escape.

His plan carried a certain level of risk. Reyes had delighted in telling him that Sable had given permission to shoot Castiel the moment his actions became suspicious, such as if a Cast took too long to work. But it was a risk Castiel was willing to take.

His situation was not the same as Mother's. He would not be abandoning anyone by Transporting himself away, or splitting up a family. He had no one he loved who would be tortured as punishment for his transgression. The Dirksens had less control over him than they thought, and if the right opportunity arrived, they were about to learn that fact.

The landing party was walking up the ramp to enter the shuttle.

"You too," Reyes said to Castiel, pushing him again with a weapon.

"Enjoying yourself?" asked Castiel as he stepped onto the ramp.

"As a matter of fact, I am," said Reyes, grinning. "It's a pain in the ass to have to hang around with a loser like you. I might as well get what I can out of it."

"Don't think I won't forget this, Reyes Dirksen," said Castiel.

"Oh, I'm sure you won't forget it. You'll just never be able to do anything about it."

They walked into the shuttle's interior. Reyes made Castiel sit down in a seat at the back of the vessel. The rest of the party took their seats too, and Kee went into the pilot's cabin. The shuttle doors didn't close, and after a few minutes, Castiel and everyone else was looking around, wondering what was causing the delay.

Footsteps sounded on the shuttle's ramp, and Sable Dirksen entered. Despite his hatred of the head of the Dirksen clan, Castiel was forced to admit she looked sublime. She was wearing a calf-length dress heavily brocaded in threads made from precious metals. Iridescent gemstones studded the fabric, and the choker around her neck seemed to be made from the shell of a rare mollusk. Castiel remembered his father giving his mother a hair comb made from the same, extremely expensive material, and flying into a rage when she wasn't delighted with her gift.

"Don't look at her," Reyes hissed. "You aren't fit

to kiss her feet."

Castiel saw the look in his guard's eyes and recognized his own lust and covetousness toward Sable Dirksen. He smirked. The chances of Reyes Dirksen possessing her were probably little better than his own.

Sable passed them by without a glance and disappeared into the pilot's cabin. The shuttle doors closed and the vessel took off.

Castiel guessed that Sable had decided she would also form part of the 'diplomatic mission' to Pirine. Perhaps she wanted to be on hand if and when his mage siblings were captured. He doubted that would actually happen. There was no guarantee they had ever come to Pirine, and if they had, Carina was smart enough to keep them all hidden.

Sable could not remain on Pirine forever. Eventually she would have to concede defeat and depart.

These combined realizations made Castiel's heart sink. If no sign of mages could be found on the planet, it was unlikely he would be called upon to Cast. He would never be allowed access to elixir, and he would never have the opportunity to escape.

He would remain a prisoner indefinitely. Perhaps Sable would never require him to Cast. Perhaps she would take him back to Ostillon and lock him away in a cell deep under the mountain castle, along with Calvaley. If Castiel were in Sable's position, that is probably what he would do.

She had spoken of mages as threats and

liabilities, and, after all, at the end of the day he would always be a Sherrerr.

"Thinking about what you're going to do to find your sister?" asked Reyes, leaning uncomfortably into Castiel's shoulder.

Castiel didn't deign to answer.

"I would, if I were you," said Reyes. "If I were you," he repeated, "I would make myself as useful as possible. Otherwise we might see no reason for keeping you alive."

Castiel stared doggedly ahead at the seatback in front of him. Would the Dirksens actually execute him? He hadn't considered that. The notion that someone would or could put an end to his life was too detestable to contemplate. Yet now that Reyes had brought up the possibility, Castiel could not exclude it.

His resolve to escape the Dirksens at the earliest opportunity became even more urgent. Remaining under their control was a constant threat to his liberty and his life.

The shuttle was touching down in Ulcawell Spaceport, and Sable and Kee emerged from the pilot's cabin. Kee began to address the troops and members of the *Elsinore's* crew. Sable walked directly to the back of the cabin, where Reyes and Castiel sat.

She was holding something in her hand. When Castiel recognized it, dismay coursed through him.

"Reyes, put these on his wrist and your own," said Sable.

Reyes took the handcuffs and did as he'd been instructed, closing one band around his left wrist and one around Castiel's right.

"Right," said Sable, giving Reyes a metal fob that Castiel assumed was the unlocking device. "You're both to accompany Kee. Do whatever he says. And if Castiel tries to escape, shoot to kill, remember?"

"Yes, ma'am."

"I would rather have the filthy little traitor dead than working against us." Sable shot Castiel a glance filled with disgust before leaving them.

"Not going far now, huh?" asked Reyes, lifting his left arm.

Castiel's right arm was dragged upward by the cuffs. Their appearance had certainly made things more difficult for him. If he did manage to Cast Transport without being shot, Reyes would be coming along.

CHAPTER TWENTY-THREE

Carina and her family had found a street that petered out at the edge of the city, and they stepped from the prairie onto the dust road. Their priority was to find somewhere they could all sleep that night. Carina planned on leaving Parthenia in charge while she and Bryce went out to look for work.

The wages they would receive for the low-level jobs they might expect to find would be small , and they had five children to feed as well as themselves. That would place a considerable delay on Carina's plan to return to Ostillon and face up to Castiel. It would take a long time to save enough for passage to the planet, yet there wasn't anything Carina could do about it. Protecting her siblings came first.

The suburb the mages had entered was old and unkempt. Carina found this a little odd. Usually, newer buildings were found at the edge of metropolises. That was where expansion took place. On the other hand, Pirine was not a rich, quickly developing place as Ostillon had been.

Until she could afford to buy an interface, they would have to rely on face-to-face encounters to find lodging and work. Carina's fingers closed around the local currency Jace had given her, which was tucked into her pocket. All they needed was a room and bathroom. A kitchen would be good too. Cooking at home was usually cheaper than buying street food.

"Should we knock at someone's door and ask if they know anyone who has a place to rent?" Parthenia asked.

"Let's walk a few more streets into the city," said Carina.

They passed along the wide roads, lined with trees and one-story houses. It was not the kind of neighborhood where Carina would expect to find rental places. The area was somewhere that families lived, children growing up and playing in the large yards.

As they walked, Carina remembered a similar search on Ostillon, trying to find work and a place to stay. She also recalled Reyes Dirksen and his convoluted plan to return her to his mother's clutches. At the time, his assertions that he'd planned on leaving the Dirksens had seemed convincing. Perhaps he'd been genuinely considering the idea. But loyalty to his family had won out in the end.

"I'm tired," Oriana announced. "I want to sit down. Riding on that horse hurt my bottom."

"Oriana," said Ferne, exasperation edging his tone, "stop complaining. We're all tired."

"I'm only saying," his sister replied, indignant.

"We could ask at one of these houses if they know somewhere we can stay," said Parthenia.

Carina didn't hold out much hope but it wouldn't hurt to try. They had walked a few hundred meters into the city.

"Okay," she said. "I'll ask. You all wait here."

While the children clustered on the sidewalk Carina strode to the nearest home and looked into the security panel. If anyone was home their house system would notify them they had a visitor. She waited.

A minute later, the door opened. A short, old woman stood in the doorway and removed buds from her ears. "Yes?"

"Sorry for disturbing you," said Carina. "We're looking for somewhere to stay." She glanced at her siblings and saw them through an outsider's eyes: dusty, disheveled, and needy looking. How different from the rich, privileged children she had first met. They had descended to a level of society very familiar to her. "I was wondering if you might be able to point us in the direction of a place to rent?"

The old woman's gaze took in Carina, Bryce, and the boys and girls in one brief look. "You won't find anything like that around here. You need to go into the city center."

"Okay, thanks," said Carina. She turned and stepped down from the porch.

As she returned to her waiting family, she shook her head, but then the old woman called out, "Hey, wait a minute. Come back."

When Carina reached the porch again, the

woman said, "How much are you willing to pay? I have a spare room. It isn't much, but you could put a couple of mattresses on the floor."

Carina had no idea how much to offer. She named a sum that seemed fair for a week's rent. When the woman's eyes widened and she quickly accepted, Carina realized she'd suggested too much. "Could I see the room first?" If it was tiny or awful, she would back out of the deal.

The old woman introduced herself as Bridget and invited Carina into the house. "I'm Tamira," Carina said. "Most people call me Tammy." She doubted that Castiel would have made his way to Pirine to look for them, but the precaution wouldn't hurt. She would tell the children to make up fake names as well. She hoped Darius would remember to use them.

The room was not tiny or awful. It was large and clean, though Bridget had used it as a storeroom. "I can move that stuff out in a jiffy," she said. "What do you think?"

Carina thought that as somewhere they could stay for the next week while they got on their feet, the room would do fine. She told Bridget she would take it. "But we don't have any mattresses. Will it bother you if we sleep on the floor?"

"Makes no difference to me," said Bridget. "You can swing from the ceiling for all I care."

As Carina walked through the house again on her way to tell her family the good news, she saw that Bridget's furniture was old and threadbare, and the place had not been decorated for many years. She felt less bad about over-estimating her offer for the rent. The woman could clearly use the money.

"Are you wilderfolk?" Bridget asked before Carina stepped through the front door.

"Wilderfolk?" asked Carina.

Bridget looked down, embarrassed. "I'm sorry. I don't mean to pry."

"It's okay, but I don't know what you're talking about."

"Are you from the group camping out on the prairie right now?"

"We…." Carina didn't see any reason to lie, and she couldn't think up a credible background story at such short notice. "Yes, we are. Is that what people call us?"

"We do. I hope you don't think that's rude."

"No, it's fine." Carina's curiosity was piqued. "What do people say about us?"

"Only that you all seem to meet up every few years, here on Pirine or somewhere nearby. You gather and live in a camp for a few months, and then you go. No one knows why for sure, though I've heard some rumors. Not that I believe them, of course. People love to gossip and think the worst of everyone, don't they? I'm sure you're all fine folk, just going about your business. Nothing wrong with that."

It would have been impossible for the Pirinians not to notice several hundred people gathering in an encampment for months, but Carina hadn't considered how the Matching might be perceived by outsiders. Should she Send to Jace to tell him what she'd learned?

Carina realized she couldn't if she wanted to. She didn't have anything of his to Locate him. The money he'd given her would be imprinted with the human trace of many hands. Anyway, she decided, Jace and the rest of the mage council were probably aware of the mages' image as 'wilderfolk.' It seemed harmless enough.

"I'll go and tell my family to come in," Carina said.

Oriana was delighted with the news that she didn't have to walk any farther. She and the rest of Carina's family followed her into Bridget's home. The old woman was already moving things out of her spare room. Carina and Bryce offered to help her, while the children opened the bags the young mages at the Matching had given them and began to take out blankets and other donated possessions.

Soon, the room was empty of Bridget's stored boxes, which she had crammed into spare corners of her home. From what Carina could tell, Bridget seemed to live alone. She guessed the old woman might have been tempted by the idea of some company as well as the rent money.

Carina watched her brothers and sisters as they unpacked and made themselves at home, gabbling noisily and bantering with each other. Company was certainly something Carina could provide, in spades.

Then she noticed Oriana wasn't helping. She sat in a corner, her arms folded and her lips in a pout.

Ferne asked, "What is wrong with you, Oriana? Why won't you help?"

"I don't like this place," she replied. "I want to go back out on the prairie. I don't want to live in a house. I liked our tent and living with all the mages. It isn't fair."

Carina rolled her eyes. Oriana was turning into a real pain in the ass. Something would have to be done about that, but if the girl's spoilt entitlement was the worst Carina had to face, she would be happy to settle for it.

CHAPTER TWENTY-FOUR

Castiel peered at the feed from the spy drone, amazed by what he saw. He was sitting in a room at the hotel suite the local government had assigned to the Dirksen delegation, watching a scene that was opening entirely new avenues of discovery about the world of mages.

Reyes was restless as he sat beside him, joined to Castiel's wrist by handcuffs. Castiel smiled. After nearly a week on Pirine, Reyes seemed to have entirely lost his smug delight at being Castiel's guard. The knowledge brought Castiel a modicum of pleasure. It was one of his few sources of happiness in his current situation.

Reyes had been ruthless and exacting in his performance of his duties. The only times he would take off the handcuffs were when Castiel needed to use the bathroom, and then he fastened the other cuff to a pipe before going outside to wait.

Within a couple of days the metal bands had begun to chafe both their wrists. Reyes pulled down his sleeve to act as a buffer—doing nothing to help Castiel, naturally—but it was clear that the cuff continued to irritate him.

After all, as long as Castiel was fastened to Reyes, Reyes was fastened to Castiel. Reyes might have the freedom to dictate where they went and what they did, to an extent, but he was almost as equally inconvenienced and restricted. He took out his frustration on Castiel through insults and taunts, though the mean words did not seem to make him feel any better.

Castiel had found he could bear it all if he clung on to the notion that Reyes was suffering almost as much as himself.

Then the news had arrived that the landing party might have found the mages, and the possibility had thrown a new light on everything.

Only, they hadn't apparently found *Castiel's* mages, but *some* mages. Rather a lot of them.

Commander Kee got the credit for the discovery. When he and the rest of the landing party had put out feelers, asking about strangers from outsystem who had arrived recently, specifically a young woman with five children, the answers that came back were entirely unexpected.

No one remembered seeing that particular group, but the local gossip was full of news that a gathering of 'wilderfolk' was going on, out on the prairie, and that people had been arriving for weeks in one way or another. No one minded nor did anything about it except to speculate what they were doing. The land was public, and the wilderfolk did no harm. They were expected to leave the place undamaged as they always did.

Anyone else might have ignored the information as irrelevant. Castiel certainly thought so the first time he heard it. What could possibly be interesting or useful about a group of vagrants setting up camp, probably in order to abuse brain-destroying drugs and perform weird rituals? But Kee did not seem to dismiss any information until he knew it to be worthless.

The commander had inquired more about this group and sent out soldiers dressed in civilian clothes to try to enter the camp. The attempt only brought more questions. There was no road to the campsite. The wilderfolk seemed to have walked for a day or more through long prairie grass to reach it, though there were no tracks.

So Kee had sent in the spy drones, and that was when everything had been blown out of the water.

Castiel never tired of watching the feed from the tiny drones, which looked like flies. He had never seen so many mages all in one place at once. He had never even imagined so many existed. Mother had always avoided talking about anything to do with mages unless Father forced her. Consequently, Castiel's knowledge of them was sparse.

He had formed the impression that Casting was something done rarely and for special purposes, yet the images from the encampment showed people starting fires, Transporting objects or themselves, Rising water from a spring, and performing other Casts as if it were the most ordinary behavior in the world.

"Your sister led us to a nest of mages," Reyes sneered. "You should be proud."

"Bullshit," Castiel replied. "We don't even know if she's on Pirine, let alone at that campsite. No reports have come in about her."

"She's here," said Reyes. "I'd bet money on it. It's only a matter of time until she turns up."

"I doubt it. If she's on Pirine, where is she?" Castiel asked, nodding toward the screen that displayed the drone feed. "We've seen hours of recordings now and no one's spotted her."

"Unless you have, and you're lying."

"Why would I lie?" asked Castiel. "Why would I want to protect her?"

"Yeah, you're right," said Bryce. "I was forgetting what a sniveling little squealer you are. You wouldn't piss on your family if it was on fire."

Castiel couldn't think of a suitable comeback, so he only said, "You know what Carina looks like, and the rest of them too. If any of my siblings were there you would have seen them by now."

Kee came into the room. Sable was with him. Castiel hadn't seen her for days, while she and Barrett had been attending meetings with the Pirinian governments. Sable's garb had reverted to its usual expensive simplicity.

Kee turned off the drone feed and addressed the room.

"We have received permission from the Pirinians to round up the mages and deport them. However, what we're actually going to do is surround the encampment overnight and move in at dawn, killing as many as we can. Realistically, taking into account these people's special abilities, we can't expect to wipe them all out, but we should be able to make a serious dent in their numbers and make them think twice about ever interfering in Dirksen business. The rest of the company is on its way down from the *Elsinore* as I speak."

Killing as many as we can? It was to be a massacre. The deliberate, controlled mass murder of unarmed people who had committed no crimes and had no clan affiliation. Castiel had thought Kee was somewhat soft-hearted. That was what his interrogation techniques had seemed to indicate. It appeared that impression had been incorrect.

Reyes shifted in his seat beside Castiel. When Castiel looked at the older boy, Reyes had turned pale. Was he shocked? Even Castiel himself was surprised by the viciousness of Kee's plan. The commander certainly didn't pull his punches. Or had the idea been Sable's? She wasn't the head of the clan for nothing.

Kee went on to explain the finer points of the operation, which was to take place at sunrise the following day. Castiel wondered what he and Reyes were supposed to be doing while all this bloodshed went on, but Kee did not say.

The commander was in the middle of stating the importance of separating the mages from their elixir at all costs, when Sable raised a hand to her ear and frowned. She had heard some news. Her features brightened with uncharacteristic glee.

She placed a hand on Kee's arm, signaling him to stop. She whispered in his ear, and then swiftly strode from the room.

Kee's dark eyes focused on Castiel, and he gave a small smile. "You're in luck, Castiel Sherrerr," he said. "We've found Carina and the rest of your sisters and brothers. I think it's time you had a family reunion."

CHAPTER TWENTY-FIVE

Bridget had been kind enough to cook them all dinner that evening, so Carina and Bryce didn't have to leave the house to buy food. The old woman wouldn't even accept the money that Carina offered her. In fact, she'd seemed embarrassed that Carina wanted to pay, and Carina had wondered if she'd violated a cultural expectation, perhaps insulting Bridget with her offer. It was always hard to navigate the social norms when visiting a new planet.

They were too many to fit around Bridget's small table, so they ate in their room, sitting cross-legged on the cloths the other mages had given them. The children had also discovered light, metallic bowls, plates, and cutlery among the offerings. The generosity of the young mages at the Matching gave Carina a twinge of regret. Had she done the right thing to leave, taking Darius with her? Would the current gathering be the last in the history of mages? She rubbed her forehead to ease the headache she'd had for hours.

"What's wrong?" Bryce asked before popping a spoonful of Bridget's delicious stew into his mouth.

"Just wondering if we should be doing this."

"No, we shouldn't," Oriana said. "But it isn't too late to change our minds. We could Transport back to the camp right now if we wanted to. We all know where it is."

"Don't be stupid," said Ferne. "What would Bridget think if she came in to find an empty room when no one has gone out of the door?"

"Well we don't have to leave like that," Oriana retorted. "We could leave in the morning. Go somewhere quiet where no one can see us."

"No," said Parthenia. "We have to return to Ostillon. We have to find Castiel and stop him from helping the Dirksens."

"Maybe I should go back to Magda, Carina," Darius said, concern written in his big, brown eyes.

"Ugh, we aren't going anywhere," said Carina, recalling guiltily that she had not allowed her brother the opportunity to say goodbye to his teacher and mentor.

Her headache was pounding and the split in her family's opinions was making it worse. If anything was clear, it was that they had to stay together and have a common purpose. Their time at the Matching had only served to divide everyone. "We have a plan and we're sticking to it."

"*You* have a plan, more like," said Oriana.

Ferne poked her in the ribs, and she shoved him in the chest with the heel of her hand.

"Stop it!" Carina snapped.

"Come on, kids," said Bryce. "Knock it off. Things aren't going to be easy for the next few months. We need to make a special effort to be nice and get along."

Ferne and Oriana looked daggers at each other, but they stopped fighting. However, Oriana pushed her spoon into her bowl and put the bowl down. "I've had enough." She stood up and walked to a corner of the room, where she began to make herself a bed on the floor.

"Don't worry," Bryce said softly to Carina. "She'll come around."

Oriana overheard and narrowed her eyes at him. She viciously plumped up a cushion and threw it down.

The small spat left everyone out of sorts. The rest of their dinner was eaten in silence except for the scraping of spoons. Ferne finished Oriana's stew, and when everyone had eaten, Parthenia offered to take the utensils to the kitchen to wash. Nahla went with her.

The sight of the little girl trotting alongside her older sister, her arms full of dirty bowls, warmed Carina's heart. She was so glad she'd gone to extract Nahla from her brother's clutches. How odd it was that the sibling who had once had the closest relationship with Castiel had turned out to be the least trouble to anyone.

While Parthenia and Nahla were filling Bridget's kitchen washer, the old woman came into the bedroom. "Is everything all right? Will you be turning in for the night soon?"

"Yes," Carina answered. "It's been a long day." And she and Bryce would have a long day tomorrow, looking for work. She would have to talk to Parthenia about how she would keep the children occupied. Maybe she could help them practice their Casting, providing Bridget wasn't around.

"I hope you sleep well," Bridget said. "It won't be very comfortable, lying on the floor. I wish I had something I could lend you, but I don't have anything."

"Don't worry about it, please," said Carina. "We're used to it."

Bridget left them and a few minutes later Parthenia and Nahla were back with their clean utensils. Everyone prepared to go to sleep.

Realistically, Carina realized, the children would have to find ways to contribute to the household budget if the family was to ever leave Pirine. She recalled the years she'd spent helping Nai Nai gather and polish beautiful stones to sell. It hadn't been an easy life but at the time she hadn't known any different so it hadn't seemed so bad.

The same could not be said for her sisters and brothers. But they would manage. Even Oriana would get over herself eventually. No matter how hard things got, at least they would have each other.

Oriana had already lain down, her back to everyone. Carina helped the others to fix up their beds. In truth, the hard floor of the room wouldn't be as comfortable as the compressed prairie grass under their tent at the Matching, but they would be okay. Everything would be okay.

***

Carina was sound asleep, her head on Bryce's

shoulder, when light and noises wakened her. She opened her eyes and found herself looking into a muzzle. She drew in a sharp breath and stiffened. For a moment, she thought she was having a nightmare, but no, she was awake, and what was happening was very, very real.

"Don't move," said the soldier at the other end of the weapon.

Assuming the order didn't apply to her eyes, Carina's gaze roved the room. Another soldier stood next to the first, pointing a weapon in the direction of Bryce's head. From the tenseness of his muscles, Carina guessed he was already awake.

Carina squinted toward the door and was entirely unsurprised to see Castiel standing in the doorway. What did surprise her was that Reyes was with him, and that the two were handcuffed to each other. This fact threw Carina into confusion. Was Reyes guarding Castiel, or vice versa, and why?

"Get up," said a voice to her left. Another soldier had spoken, presumably to Parthenia or Darius. Both of them had been lying on that side of Carina when they'd all gone to sleep.

Carina heard movement and the sound of quiet sobs. *Darius. Fuck.*

"I hope you're happy, taking a six year old prisoner," Carina said to Castiel.

The soldier knocked Carina's forehead with the muzzle. "Shut up."

Carina had been expecting some kind of gloating retort or at the very least a smirk from Castiel, but she got nothing. The Dark Mage looked gloomy. Reyes' expression was even gloomier.

What was going on?

"Your turn," Carina's guard said.

She slowly rose to her feet, taking in the room with her improved vantage point. Bryce stood up beside her, ordered to by his guard. Parthenia and Darius also had a guard each, and so did Nahla and Ferne. That made six soldiers in total. The Dirksens were clearly taking no chances.

The men and women were armed but not wearing armor, Carina noted, trying to figure out how the hell she could help her family escape. She needed to do something, and soon. Once they were all locked away somewhere it would be much harder to regain their freedom.

The soldiers had already found the weapons Jace had given them. The bag was open and next to the door, its contents plain to see. The elixir supplies were out of reach, and even if Carina managed to reach them, there was the eternal problem of the lag. She would be dead before she could Cast.

Darius' guard was searching him, roughly patting down the little boy as if he were an arch criminal who would pull a knife on them at any moment. Satisfied that Darius wasn't about to murder anyone right then, the soldier moved to Carina while Parthenia's guard covered her and her brother.

The soldier's hands were thorough as he felt her body, but she wasn't carrying anything useful on her person. She'd mistakenly thought they were relatively safe in Bridget's home. The old woman must have betrayed them. Her embarrassment when Carina had offered to pay for their food suddenly made more sense. Bridget must have made the call by then.

Had the local authorities issued an alert about a 'wilderfolk' family coming in from the prairie? Maybe they'd offered a reward. The old woman seemed poor enough to be easily bribed.

It was Bryce's turn to be searched.

"I'm sorry, Carina," said Reyes.

Castiel stared at him.

"Sorry?" Carina asked. "Sorry for what? For imprisoning children? For subjecting us all to a life of captivity and slavery? Or maybe for something else? I'd love to hear which of the hundreds of thousands of crimes your clan has perpetrated that you're sorry for."

"I thought it was all necessary, for the greater good, you know?' Reyes could not meet Carina's gaze. "I had no idea what my clan was capable of. I've been naive. I understand that now."

She shook her head in disgust. "Please, spare me." Then she added, "If you feel so bad, why not let us go? There's still time. Order these soldiers to release us."

"I can't do that," Reyes replied. "They aren't operating under my orders. I'm only here as an observer."

"The Dirksens plan to kill all the mages," said Castiel, sneering. "That's what's eating him up. Even *I* think that's excessive, and I guess that's saying something."

"They...what?" asked Parthenia. Her mouth hung open and her cheeks lost their color.

"It's nearly dawn, so they'll be starting soon," said Castiel. "Out at that camp on the prairie. You must know it. That's why you're here, right? Sable Dirksen and Kee found out all about it yesterday. They plan to send a clear message to mages to never use their powers against them."

"But why?" asked Parthenia, horror in her voice. "Why would they think mages would harm them? Mages only ever do good."

"I beg to differ," said Castiel, smirking.

"This is your fault," yelled Parthenia. "You've made the Dirksens feel threatened by whatever it is you've done. If any one of those mages die you'll have blood on your hands."

"Make her be quiet," Castiel said to the soldiers, but they ignored him. "Anyway," he continued, "let's not forget who started this. It was you who did all that Casting for Father, helping him with all those business deals. That was what first alerted the Dirksens to our existence. They've feared our powers since then."

"That was because he made me!" Parthenia exclaimed.

Carina was struggling to absorb the news that the mages at the Matching were about to be attacked. All the young women and men, Justin, Jace, Magda—they could all die. Of course, as soon as they realized what was happening, they would be able to Transport themselves away, but there was bound to be a lot of bloodshed.

Carina was also confused about Castiel's place among the Dirksens. He seemed to have no status, if their soldiers didn't follow his orders.

"What are you doing?" she asked him. "Why are

you here?"

"I'm to make sure none of you Casts," Castiel replied. "Not that I really give a shit. Not anymore."

So Castiel was in Reyes' custody. And Reyes was undergoing a moment of remorse. Carina wondered if she could exploit the situation somehow. Maybe there was a chance they could escape.

Then it hit her. Where was Oriana?

The revelation came as such a shock that Carina swung around to check that her sister really was missing.

"Keep still," her guard barked, and swiped the side of her head with the muzzle of his gun.

The crack dazed her.

"Hey, leave her alone," shouted Bryce. His guard thrust his weapon into his chest.

Carina felt blood trickle down her face. Where had Oriana gone?

CHAPTER TWENTY-SIX

Oriana listened to the sound of everyone's breathing. One by one, most of her sisters and brothers had fallen asleep, and so had Bryce. Only Carina had remained awake. Now, finally, Oriana heard her eldest sister's breaths become deep and regular like the others'.

She would wait another five minutes or so and then she would leave. While she waited, Oriana remembered the nights she had snuck out of her room at night, when she'd lived on Ithiya and Mother and Father had been alive. Those secret nocturnal excursions around the mansion and into the garden had been the only times she'd felt truly alone. No servants had been watching her, surreptitiously or not. Father had not been silently judging her with his cold eyes. Mother had not been regarding her, pain and sorrow in every look.

In those brief times she had wandered Father's estate in the dead of night, when the entire household slept, Oriana had felt free. It had been an illusion, of course. None of them had been free, not even Father. He had been a slave to his pride, arrogance, and ambition.

Was what she planned to do due to pride or arrogance? No. She only wanted to be free. She wanted to choose her own life. She had been through enough hard times. She deserved to make her own decisions on how she lived.

Oriana slowly sat up and pushed down her blanket. Ferne was sound asleep, dribbling like he always did, the starlight through the window lighting up his face. Everyone else was shadowy lumps in the darkness.

She had already thought out her list of what she needed to take. Clothes, elixir, her brush and toothbrush, and a couple of blankets. That would be all she would need. She had packed a bag while she'd been getting ready for bed. No one had even noticed what she was doing.

A sense of self-satisfaction warmed her. She had made careful preparations. She wasn't a silly little girl, running away for no reason. She had made a decision maturely, and now she was going to act on it.

Oriana stood up, picking up her filled bag from the floor. She also picked up her shoes in the other hand. She would put them on when she was outside the house so the noise of her footsteps wouldn't wake anyone up.

As she took a last look at her family and Bryce, something tugged at her heart, causing a sharp pain. Would she see her brothers and sisters again? She didn't know, but she hoped so.

Don't be silly, she told herself. *Of course you'll*

see them again. They'll all attend the Matching eventually. You can see them there.

Feeling a little better, Oriana tiptoed across the room with its sleeping figures around the edges, eased open the door, and stepped through it. She closed the door, leaving it slightly ajar to avoid making any noise. The hall was very dark, but she could see light through a window in the door. Hoping that the woman who owned the house didn't set her security system to monitor internal movement, Oriana walked along the hall, opened the front door, and slipped out.

She guessed it had to be the early hours of the morning. Lights were on in the distant city center, but the only lights she could see by were the handful of dim streetlights that lined the road.

Oriana shivered. The coldness and dampness of the night was already invading her bones. She looked up and down the street. Would anyone see her if she Transported right then and there? Probably not, but there was no sense in taking chances. She needed to go somewhere she could not be observed.

She walked along the sidewalk, heading back toward the prairie. She imagined how nice it would be to live among the young mages again, carefree and happy. At the campsite she didn't have to hide what she was or live in constant fear of discovery and capture.

Someone would take pity on her and accept her into their family, she was sure. Perhaps that nice ranger, Jace, from Ostillon. On the other hand, that wasn't such a good idea. Castiel was on Ostillon, and he was the one member of her family she did not want to meet again.

It didn't really matter who she ended up with. All the mages were nice and kind. She would find someone. She wouldn't have to live the lifetime of hardship Carina seemed intent upon.

Oriana scanned the road from side to side, trying to find somewhere that was not overlooked. In a few minutes' time she would be back at the prairie and her new life would begin.

CHAPTER TWENTY-SEVEN

Carina saw Castiel watching her, amusement in his eyes. *He knew!* He knew Oriana was missing and he hadn't said anything.

Reyes had to know too. He'd met all her brothers and sisters when she'd found them outside the spaceport on Ostillon. The only person he hadn't met was Bryce, who had appeared later.

Both Castiel and Reyes had not let on to the soldiers that the party they were taking prisoner had one extra person: Bryce, and that one of them was missing. And because there were enough guards for one per prisoner, they hadn't suspected anything.

"Carina," said Darius, "where did Oriana go?"

"Huh?" said one of the soldiers. "Who are you talking about?"

Shit!

Carina stared at her young brother, willing him to be silent. He looked back, confused, and then opened his mouth to speak again.

No, Darius! No!

Then he was gone. Vanished into thin air. Parthenia had disappeared too.

"What the fuck?" a soldier yelled. "How do they do that?"

"Never mind that," shouted another. "We have to stop them. Grab the rest."

Darius and Parthenia had been Transported. Oriana must have done it. She had to be watching them from somewhere. The only possible place was the window. Carina forced herself not to look at it.

Her guard lunged at her, trying to grab her arm. She shoved him to one side. Oriana would be preparing to Transport the others. If a soldier was holding onto one of the mages, he might Transport with them.

"Fight," Carina cried. "Push them away from you!"

She heard the hiss of a pulse round and the thump of a body hitting the floor. Carina guard reached for her again. She kicked his knee and heard a crunch. The man screamed. Carina spun around. Ferne was down! His bastard guard had fired at him.

But then Ferne was gone, and so was Nahla.

Only herself and Bryce were left. Carina's guard was rolling and groaning on the floor, but Bryce was locked in a struggle with his guard.

Castiel and Reyes stood in the doorway and did nothing.

From outside came the sound of someone shouting, "What's going on in there?"

Carina ran at the soldier holding on to Bryce.

She was within a step of him when she Transported.

***

Carina was in darkness, momentum carrying her forward. She crashed into Bryce and the soldier, and all three of them fell to the ground, hitting grass. Carina guessed they were somewhere in the yards around Bridget's house, but as she tussled with the guard who had grabbed Bryce she realized they were out on the prairie. A stiff wind was blowing, causing the tents to flap.

"Let go of him," Carina shouted, standing up to get a better look at Bryce and his assailant. The guard's weapon was trapped under him, and he was rolling around too much to punch him in the jaw. So she did the next best thing she could think of. She kicked one of his legs open and drove her heel into the man's groin as hard as she could.

That persuaded him to give up. While the guard rolled on the ground in silent agony, Bryce shook himself and stood up.

"Remind me to never piss you off," he said.

Carina relieved the guard of his weapon, and then straightened up and turned full circle. "I don't believe it."

Oriana had Transported them all back to the mages' camp. The camp that was about to be attacked. Darius, Parthenia, Ferne, and Nahla were all there too.

Carina scanned the horizon beyond the tents full of sleeping mages. A rosy patch told her dawn was about to break.

Oriana suddenly appeared, Transporting herself in. "I'm sorry, I'm so sorry," she sobbed. "I'm sorry

I ran away. I wanted to come back here. I didn't want to spend my life scraping to get by, always on the move. But then I realized I would miss you all too much. I went back to the house, and I saw soldiers, and—"

"You're sorry?" said Bryce. "You just saved all our lives."

"Not yet," said Carina. The sensible thing would be to leave right away, to Transport the hell out of that massacre waiting to happen. But there was no way she could abandon her kindred to such a terrible fate. "We have to wake everyone up."

"What?" Oriana asked. "Why?"

"The Dirksens are about to attack," said Ferne.

Oriana's eyes grew wide, and her brothers and sisters seemed frozen by the enormity of the evil about to befall the young mages at the Matching.

Carina ran to the nearest tent, ripped open the flap, and yelled, "Wake up! You're being attacked. You have to Transport away from the camp!"

"Come on, hurry," Carina said to Bryce and her siblings. "Help me."

This galvanized them into action, and they began to run to other tents.

"I'll go and tell Magda," said Darius.

"No, you won't," Carina replied. "You're staying here with me." She was not about to lose her brother to the Spirit Mage again.

And then she saw what she'd done. The camp was about to come under fire, and she had just sent her brothers and sisters away from her, where she could not protect them. They would all become separated. How would they find each other again?

"Wait!" she shouted. "Come back!" But

Parthenia and the others didn't hear her. The noise in the camp was growing louder as the young mages woke up and asked each other what was going on. Bryce had also disappeared.

Damn!

Jace. Carina needed to speak to him. Or Justin. Someone who was in charge.

The mages she had woken were not Transporting. They were standing around and chatting.

"You have to get out of here," Carina yelled at one group. "The camp is about to be attacked."

"Aren't you the one who left?" one of them asked. "The new Spirit Mage's sister?"

"Yes," Carina replied. "And I've come back to warn you, you must leave. Dirksen soldiers are about to attack and kill everyone."

"But how do you know?" the questioner asked.

"It would take too long to explain," said Carina. "You must believe me."

A scream echoed across from somewhere out at the edge of the camp, borne along on the strong breeze.

"It's begun," Carina said. "Now do you believe me?"

The mages' expressions grew frightened. One of them nodded and returned to her tent.

"Grab whatever you can, quickly," said Carina. "Take all the elixir you can carry, and Transport as far from here as possible. Hide out somewhere until it's safe to leave Pirine. But before you Transport, Send to someone else in the camp and tell them to do the same."

Carina grabbed Darius' hand. "Do you know

where Jace and Justin's tent is?"

"No. Only the Spirit Mage's."

"Ugh, then the Spirit Mage's it'll have to be."

Screams and shouts were sounding from another direction. The soldiers were closing in. Mages were already dying. Carina had to try to save as many as she could, but she knew she couldn't do it alone. By the time everyone received a warning the soldiers would be halfway through the camp.

In fact, now that she thought about it, the Spirit Mage was exactly the person she needed to see.

When Carina and Darius burst into the old woman's tent, she was sound asleep despite the increasing mayhem going on around her. Carina grabbed Magda's shoulder and roughly shook it.

"Be gentle, Carina," said Darius. "She's very old."

"I know, but..." Carina bit her lip. Without the Spirit Mage's help, hundreds of people would die.

The rheumy eyes opened and blinked blearily. "What...? Carina, my dear. You came back."

A scream of protest, suddenly cut off, came through the walls of the tent.

"What was that?" Magda asked.

Carina said, "Can you Send to everyone in the camp? You Summoned them all, right? Can you Send to them? It's very important."

"Yes, I...." She sat up, pushing down the blankets that covered her. "What's happening?"

"The Dirksens are attacking, and they plan on killing every mage they find."

Magda's mouth gaped. She looked at Darius.

"It's true," he said.

"Bring me my elixir," said Magda.

Darius had already grabbed it. He handed the Spirit Mage the canister and she removed the lid. "Do it with me, Darius," she said. "I'll need your help. You know how." After Darius nodded his agreement, she added, "Drink half of it. You'll need it."

Between them, Magda and Darius drank the entire canister of elixir. Then they held hands and closed their eyes.

All around, the sounds of fear, dismay, and confusion were rising, bubbling up like water in the spring at the center of the encampment. But Carina could hear another sound: a muted, rustling roar. She couldn't figure out what it was.

Magda and Darius unclasped their hands. As Magda opened her eyes, her skin increased in pallor. She looked exhausted.

"I've done my best," she said. "I cannot do any more right now."

Darius also looked tired.

Then Carina suddenly recognized the sound that had been puzzling her. It was fire. The Dirksens had set the camp on fire.

Rather than go from tent to tent, they were trying to drive out all the mages into the open, where the soldiers could pick them off, like hunters shooting game. Carina felt as though she was about to vomit.

"Can we go and find Parthenia and the others now?" Darius asked.

"Yes," Carina said. Then a thought struck her. "Darius, can you Send to them, even though you don't have anything of theirs? The same as you did just now to the mages in the camp?"

His little face brightened. "Yes, I can!" But then his features darkened again. "But not to Bryce or Nahla."

"It's okay, we can find them. Tell the others to come here, to the Spirit Mage's tent."

While waiting for Darius to Cast, Carina said to Magda, "You should leave. It isn't safe anywhere in the camp now. The soldiers will be here soon." *Or the fire will reach you.*

"No," the Spirit Mage replied. "My place is here. Until everyone has gone. My role is to save magehood for the future and I will do that to my last breath."

"But you're the repository of our history," Carina said. "If you die, our history dies with you."

"Our history did not seem so important to you yesterday," said Magda, her eyes twinkling. "You have a lot to learn, Carina. If I run out on my people, there's no point in me remembering anything."

Carina did not have time to argue with the old woman. She knew what she was doing. "Did you Send to the others?" Carina asked Darius.

"I did."

"Right. Let's go."

"Wait," said Magda. "Take some elixir with you, or you won't be able to Transport yourselves out."

Carina grabbed canisters for herself and Darius, and ran out of the tent.

The sky was red. The hues were from the rising sun and the burning encampment. Smoke and flames were billowing upward in the far reaches of the camp, but the breeze was blowing the fire closer every second.

Somewhere out there were Ferne, Parthenia, and Oriana, hopefully now heading toward the Spirit Mage's tent. Carina would have to find Bryce and Nahla. How, she didn't know yet. On the plus side, mages were Transporting away from the site. Carina could see them leave their tents, clutching bags, and then disappearing. She could also see shadowy moving forms inside tents, back-lit by the glow of flames, vanish from sight.

"Darius," said Carina, "I'm going to Transport you to the…." Where could she send her brother that would be safe?

"No," said Darius. "I want to stay with you."

Carina was forced to acquiesce, as she could not think of a place on Pirine where Darius could wait for her in safety. "Okay. But stick to me like glue. Don't leave my side."

Darius gripped her hand, and they set off. As soon as Carina found Bryce and Nahla, they would return to Magda's tent to rendezvous with the others, and then they would all leave together. Carina didn't think there was anything else she could do to help the stricken mages. Though she carried the guard's weapon, she could not fight off tens, perhaps hundreds, of soldiers by herself.

Holding Darius' hand tightly, Carina ran along an avenue of tents. She shouted to the remaining mages to leave immediately, driving home Magda and Darius' message. They were running toward the flames, but Carina couldn't help it. The soldiers had set fire to the camp on all sides. Danger lay in every direction.

Where was Bryce? Where was Nahla?

Someone was heading in their direction. Carina recognized her sister. "Parthenia!" she shouted. Her sister had Nahla with her! If there had been time, Carina would have kissed her. "Don't stop," she said. "Go to Magda's and wait for us. If you see any soldiers or the fire comes near, Transport to the trail we followed on the horses. About halfway along."

Parthenia nodded and Carina's two sisters ran past her.

Her heart lightening a fraction, she ran on. The campsite was beginning to look deserted. Carina hoped the majority of the mages had gotten away. The Dirksens would scour the planet for them, of course, but if the young men and women were careful, they stood a good chance of not being captured.

Carina and Darius were nearing the flames. She didn't dare to move any closer, yet there was no sign of Bryce. She guessed he must have gone to another area. If she didn't find him soon, the entire place would be ablaze.

Worse still, the roaring of the flames made it impossible to hear pulse rounds being fired. She had no idea if troops were approaching.

"Jace!" Darius screamed. He was staring off to one side, his hand like a vise on Carina's.

When she saw what her brother was looking at, her heart froze. A pillar of fire was stumbling between the tents. Was it Jace? Carina could not tell if it was him or his brother. The mage must have stayed behind after Magda's warning, to ensure the young mages Transported. The flames had overtaken him.

And that wasn't all. A soldier was emerging behind him in heat-resistant armor. His head covered in a specialized helmet and carrying an oxygen mix tank on his backs, the soldier took aim at Jace, preparing to finish him off. But Carina's weapon was already at her shoulder and spitting pulse rounds at the man. She didn't release her trigger until he was down.

Darius was fumbling with the lid of his elixir, tears streaming down his face.

"There isn't anything you can do," Carina said. She didn't know a Cast that would extinguish flames, and even if she did, Jace was already too burned to survive.

"Yes, there is!" Darius shouted. "Please help me, Carina."

Still doubtful, Carina unscrewed Darius' canister and held it to his lips. The small boy swallowed a mouthful of elixir.

Too late. It was too late.

Carina could not bear to imagine the agony Jace was in. Perhaps it would have been kinder to allow the soldier to shoot him. Perhaps it would be kinder to do it herself.

She couldn't watch. If Darius put out the flames, what would they do then?

"I did it," Darius announced.

Carina looked. The man was on the ground. The flames had gone out. By some miracle, Carina's brother had invented a new Cast to douse fire. Should she have let him? "Stay behind me," she said. "And don't look, okay?"

Jace was still alive. His burned body moved slowly on charred grass as Carina approached him.

Fuck. What had she done? He was dying. He deserved a quicker death.

Darius peeked from behind Carina and gasped at what he saw. Nevertheless, he said, "I can Heal him."

"I told you not to look," Carina said. "And, no you can't. You can't Heal a fatal condition. I think I'm going to have to...." She fingered the trigger of her weapon. How would she explain to Darius what she had to do?

"You cannot Heal him, Darius," Magda said, "but I can." Carina swung around and saw the Spirit Mage. The old woman had Transported there, somehow knowing what had happened.

The Spirit Mage knelt down next to Jace and gently touched his burned skin. She opened her flask and drank elixir before she began to Cast.

Carina didn't know if Magda would be successful, but she also had no time to find out. She had to find Bryce and get out of there.

"Come with me," she said to Darius.

"But what about—"

"Don't argue."

Her little brother in tow, Carina fled from the grisly scene. They hadn't gone more than twenty paces, however, before Carina saw figures approaching through the flames. Soldiers. They were walking steadily forward, scanning from side to side for mages.

Carina halted. They hadn't yet seen her or Darius. There were about ten of them. The minute she shot at them they would shoot back, endangering Darius. Should she try to get out of sight or Cast Transport? Any movement was bound to catch the soldiers' attention.

In the end, the decision was made for her. Darius had spotted the troops too. He gave a shriek, ripped his hand from Carina's, and sprinted back toward Magda and Justin.

Carina had no choice except to follow him. A pulse round grazed her shoulder. They'd been spotted. Carina began to run a haphazard zigzag, desperately trying to avoid the soldiers' fire. Darius was running in a dead straight line. It was only a matter of time....

He had reached Magda and Jace, but the scene was not at all what Carina had expected. Magda was lying on her side, one arm flailed outward. Jace remained on his back, but all his burned skin had disappeared. He was Healed. He was alive.

Darius threw himself onto Magda. From the old woman's staring eyes, Carina realized she was dead. The Spirit Mage had brought Jace back to life at the sacrifice of her own.

A pulse round hit Carina square on her back. Unbearable agony spread from the wound. Carina's legs collapsed under her, and she found herself falling forward. This was no stunning blow. The soldiers' weapons were set to kill. This was the end.

Distantly, Carina could hear Darius crying out, howling in pain and grief.

"I will save you, Carina," he said. "I will Heal you."

As her life ebbed away, Carina whispered, "No. No, don't, Darius."

Not like that. Not like Magda had done.

CHAPTER TWENTY-EIGHT

When Carina opened her eyes, she looked up into a smoky sky, red with the reflected flames of a fire. The air was filled with the fire's roar and the tang of burning. Carina remembered she was on Ostillon, in the basement of a house, and the Sherrerrs were bombarding the city. She had to get everyone out, but her leg was broken.

No, that wasn't right. That had happened weeks ago. Where was she now? Suddenly, the memory of Pirine, the Matching, and everything that had happened flooded back.

"No," she shouted, trying to sit up. "No, Darius. Don't do it!"

"She's alive," exclaimed Parthenia. "Let's go."

Carina felt a firm hand grasp her wrist. "No," she repeated. "Stop him. Someone stop him." Darius had been trying to Heal her like Magda had Healed Jace. Only the Spirit Mage had died in the attempt. Darius could not give his life for hers. She wouldn't let him.

"Stay still," said Parthenia. The grip on Carina's wrist tightened. She felt herself Transported. The noise and smell of the fire was gone, and the sky was the pale pink of a natural dawn. She was lying on prairie grass.

Carina's back ached where the pulse round had hit, but she was alive. She was alive, and her little brother had died to Heal her. She could not bear it. How could she go on living? Carina turned onto her side, too anguished even to cry.

"Hey," someone said. Carina recognized Bryce's voice. She felt his hand on her shoulder. So he was okay. He'd escaped from the encampment with them. Carina was relieved, but she could not feel a flicker of happiness. She would never be happy again.

"Carina," said Bryce. "It's all right. We're going to be okay."

She closed her eyes, pressed her lips together, and shook her head. They were not.... The understanding that Parthenia and Bryce were acting far too calmly for the situation finally pierced her fears. Carina opened her eyes and sat up.

They were out on the prairie, entirely alone, the sea of tall grass stretching out around them. Parthenia had brought them to the place Carina had suggested, along the horse trail into the city. A small body lay nearby, but Carina couldn't bring herself to look at it. A terrible dread rose up in her when she tried.

Bryce was sitting next to her, his face and clothes blackened and smelling of smoke.

"Is...." Carina paused and swallowed. "Is Darius alive?"

"Yes," Bryce replied. "Of course he is. Is that what was bothering you? He's out of it, but he seems to be okay."

"Oh, thank the stars," Carina breathed. Tears of relief poured from her eyes. She crawled over to her little brother. Like Bryce and everyone else, he bore the marks of the fire, but he was otherwise unharmed and he was breathing normally.

How in the world...? Carina could not figure it out. "What happened? I only remember being shot."

"I don't know what happened to you," said Bryce. "Oriana and Ferne found me and told me we were all meeting at the Spirit Mage's tent. When we arrived there, Parthenia and Nahla were waiting, but there was no sign of the mage or you two. We hung around, figuring you would turn up eventually. I think Ferne was about to Send to you. He was going to let you know we were all ready to go and only needed you to come back, when you and Darius appeared. Darius immediately passed out, and you looked to be half dead. But then you came around. Parthenia decided it was time to get out of there, and here we are."

Carina could only guess at most of what had happened, though there was no doubt in her mind that Darius had saved her life. And apparently at great cost to himself, though not enough to kill him. Perhaps the Healing Cast had been too much for the old woman, but Darius, being younger, had survived it. He must have Transported her and himself to the Spirit Mage's tent before collapsing.

But what she could not figure out was why the soldiers had not shot her brother. They had been coming up behind her, and Darius had been right there, clearly a mage and a target to be taken out. Yet they had not shot him. Perhaps they had not been able to bring themselves to kill a little boy.

Perhaps there remained a smidgen of humanity at the heart of the most evil people.

Carina thought of Castiel. Though he'd known Oriana had gone missing, he had said nothing to the soldiers who had come to Bridget's house to take his family captive. She also thought of Reyes, who seemed to have finally comprehended the evilness of his clan.

Carina gasped. What had happened to Jace? He'd been alive when the troops had been approaching. Had they shot him or spared him like they had Darius?

"Looking for me, Carina?" said a deep voice behind her.

She swiveled around. The large man was sitting on the grass, entirely unburned and very much alive.

"I forgot," said Bryce. "Darius brought Jace with him too. I was kind of focused on you at the time."

They were all there: all her brothers and sisters, Bryce, and even Jace. But how many of the young mages had died in the Dirksens' attack?

"Do you know if most of the mages managed to get away?" Carina asked Jace.

The burly man's expression was sad as he replied, "Not all, but most, thanks to the help of your family." He paused. "It's strange how things turn out sometimes. I didn't want you to leave and take Darius from us, yet if you hadn't left, you wouldn't have found out about what the Dirksens planned to do. You wouldn't have warned us, and many more people would have been lost. So that is something to be thankful for."

"I'm sorry that Magda died," said Carina.

"So am I," said Jace. "Perhaps more than you will ever know. She was everything to us. She was our history, our culture, our future. She had barely begun to pass on all she knew to Darius. Now, I do not know what will happen. How can we continue when we've lost so much?"

Carina's heart ached with remorse and sadness. She had been so wrong about Magda. She had misinterpreted the Spirit Mage's deep need to safeguard mage lore as a desire to monopolize Darius. Carina realized how blind she had been, and now there was nothing she could do about it.

"Do not blame yourself for what has happened," said Jace, reading her expression. "The Dirksens are responsible for Magda's fate , not you."

"What should happen to Darius?" Carina asked.

"Though he is a powerful mage, Darius is very young, and he doesn't know anywhere near enough to take over as our clan's Spirit Mage. Everything has changed. A new era in magehood has begun, and I don't know what will happen to us. Perhaps it is the beginning of our end."

"Or perhaps it's the beginning of something new," said Carina. "Maybe we can find a different way of living where we no longer need to skulk and hide."

Jace looked downward and didn't answer.

"It's kind of empty and lonely out here," said

Oriana. "Are we going to leave soon? Where are we going now?"

It was a big question, both for their immediate future and their long-term plans. The first thing they had to do was to go somewhere far from the Dirksens' soldiers. But then what?

"Maybe we should head into the city," Parthenia said. "But what about returning to Ostillon eventually? Castiel might go back there."

"Castiel?" said Carina. "I don't think we need to worry about him anymore. I'm pretty sure he isn't a danger to anyone. His plan to gain power and privilege has backfired spectacularly."

"Maybe that guy, Reyes, will take care of him," said Ferne.

"They certainly didn't seem to be best buddies," Bryce remarked.

"Are we going?" Ferne asked, standing up.

He was right to hurry them. The morning was wearing on. Dirksen soldiers would be scouring the prairie, hoping to find stray mages.

Carina sighed. "Yes. Let's go where we always go: somewhere safe, out of sight, where we won't attract too much attention. Then we'll have to see what we can do to leave Pirine without any Dirksens or Sherrerrs on our tail."

"And then what?" asked Oriana.

"I'm not sure," said Carina. But in fact, she was. She had always been sure, deep down. She took a breath and said, "Maybe we should try to find Earth."

Jace gave a shake of his head. "You're chasing a dream, Carina."

"Do you have a better idea?"

"No," Jace replied. "I have to admit I don't."
"Then a dream is better than nothing."

Carina's story continues in...

Mercenary Mage

Sign up to my reader group for a free copy of the Star Mage Saga prequel, Star Mage Exile, at:

https://jjgreenauthor.com/free-books/

Reviews are essential to the success of a book. If you enjoyed *Wildfire and Steel,* please consider leaving an honest review.

ALSO BY J.J. GREEN

SHADOWS OF THE VOID

SPACE COLONY ONE

CARRIE HATCHETT, SPACE ADVENTURER

LOST TO TOMORROW

THERE COMES A TIME
A SCIENCE FICTION COLLECTION

DAWN FALCON
A FANTASY COLLECTION

First Edition.

Lightning Source UK Ltd.
Milton Keynes UK
UKHW020636130120
356857UK00011B/837/P

9 781913 476090